Check out what RT Book Reviews *is saying about Rhonda Nelson's heroes in—and out of—uniform!*

Of *Letters from Home*
"This highly romantic tale is filled with emotion and wonderful characters. It's a heart-melting romance."

Of *The Soldier*
"Wonderfully written and heart-stirring, the story flies by to the deeply satisfying ending."

Of *The Hell-Raiser*
"A highly entertaining story that has eccentric secondary characters, hot sex and a heartwarming romance."

Of *The Loner*
"A highly romantic story with two heartwarming characters and a surprise ending."

Blaze

Dear Reader,

Thank you so much for picking up *The Ranger*. It's the sixth book in my Men Out of Uniform series, and I can't tell you how much I enjoy writing these unrepentantly male badass heroes. They're all Southern gentlemen, so they know how to treat a lady—when they find the right one—and they're honest and noble to the core. Toss in a wicked sense of humor to go with an equally wicked smile and these guys are lethal. And Will Forrester is no exception....

Will's first assignment for Ranger Security, though a bit bizarre, seems harmless enough. Find Theo Watson, an elderly gentleman who is looking for the Watson family jewels, which were, according to family lore, hidden right before the Union soldiers marched on Atlanta during the Civil War (or the War of Northern Aggression as some still call it down here.) But when Rhiannon Palmer arrives on the scene determined to "help" Will, things take a completely unexpected turn and soon all Will wants to do is *help* Rhiannon...right into bed.

Be sure to look for Chase Harrison's story, "The Prodigal," in *Born on the Fourth of July* next month and Tanner Crawford's in *The Renegade* in August. Nothing warms the cockles of my heart more than hearing from my readers, so be sure to check out my Web site at www.ReadRhondaNelson.com.

Happy reading!

Rhonda

Rhonda Nelson

THE RANGER

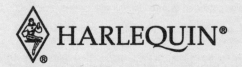

HARLEQUIN®

TORONTO • NEW YORK • LONDON
AMSTERDAM • PARIS • SYDNEY • HAMBURG
STOCKHOLM • ATHENS • TOKYO • MILAN • MADRID
PRAGUE • WARSAW • BUDAPEST • AUCKLAND

Recycling programs
for this product may
not exist in your area.

ISBN-13: 978-0-373-79549-9

THE RANGER

Copyright © 2010 by Rhonda Nelson.

ABOUT THE AUTHOR

A Waldenbooks bestselling author, two-time RITA® Award nominee and *RT Book Reviews* Reviewers' Choice nominee, Rhonda Nelson writes hot romantic comedy for the Harlequin Blaze line and other Harlequin imprints. With more than twenty-five published books to her credit and many more coming down the pike, she's thrilled with her career and enjoys dreaming up her characters and manipulating the worlds they live in. In addition to a writing career she has a husband, two adorable kids, a black Lab and a beautiful bichon frise. She and her family make their chaotic but happy home in a small town in northern Alabama. She loves to hear from her readers, so be sure to check her out at www.ReadRhondaNelson.com.

Books by Rhonda Nelson

HARLEQUIN BLAZE
172—GETTING IT GOOD!
217—GETTING IT RIGHT!
223—GETTING IT NOW!
255—THE PLAYER
277—THE SPECIALIST
283—THE MAVERICK
322—THE EX-GIRLFRIENDS' CLUB
361—FEELING THE HEAT
400—THE LONER
412—THE HELL-RAISER
475—LETTERS FROM HOME
481—THE SOLDIER

For Amy Weaver, my BFF and quintessential cool chick.

1

FORMER SOLDIER Will Forrester pushed through the double doors of the sleek Atlanta high-rise that housed Ranger Security and prepared to meet his new destiny.

For the first time in his adult life, as a civilian.

His fingers involuntarily twitched at his sides, betraying the slightest hint of unease. Though he had always thought highly of the gentlemen who'd started this company—finding better soldiers than Brian Payne, Jamie Flanagan and Guy McCann would be damned near impossible—Will had nevertheless never imagined that he'd be working for them.

In fact, if anyone had told him three months ago that he would be anything other than in service to Uncle Sam, he would have asked them to hand over their crack pipe and would personally have escorted them to rehab.

But that was before the…incident.

Will determinedly closed the door on that line of thinking before any of the horrific images could form. One, in particular, haunted him.

Knobby knees, thin limbs, a bloodied, tattered teddy bear…

He squeezed his eyes tightly shut and swore under his breath. Dammit, he had to get a grip. He couldn't afford to blow this. He had been especially grateful to Colonel Carl Garrett for making the recommendation for this new career. Frankly, when he'd decided he had to get out—that he no longer had the stomach for war—Will hadn't given much thought to where he would go or what he would do. He just knew that he couldn't do his job anymore, that he'd never be able to do it again.

As for the men who were with him that fateful day, Chase Harrison and Tanner Crawford, who knew what they were going to do? Chase seemed to be dealing with the tragedy much better then he or Tanner had, so Will figured he would ultimately continue in service. Tanner, however, was more than likely on his way out. He sincerely hoped Garrett would extend the same recommendation for Tanner that he had for him. Tanner deserved it.

On some level Will had imagined that he'd go

home to Mockingbird, Mississippi, a quaint little town nestled in the heart of the Delta. His grandmother was still there, after all. Gardening, quilting and sipping iced tea. Having lost his parents and little brother in a car accident when he was ten, Will had been raised by his paternal grandparents.

His grandmother had kept him well loved and well fed and his grandfather, who'd passed five years ago, had taught him the benefit of fewer words and more action, the advantage of hard work and patience and, of course, how to treat a lady. The thought made Will smile. God knows John Forrester had loved his "Miss Molly" and had treated her accordingly. He missed him, Will thought now, and knew his grandmother did, as well.

It felt like a lifetime ago that he'd been home, that he'd put his feet under her table and enjoyed a home-cooked meal and good company. He actually should have gone to see her before coming here, but Garrett had insisted that he was needed *now*.

Besides, his grandmother would ask probing questions—ones he didn't want to answer at present—so this was truly for the best. He'd go and see her as soon as he got this new job in order—first things first always—and he'd make sure to call more often in the interim.

"Will Forrester?" a slim, no-nonsense gentleman asked from behind a remarkably tidy desk.

Will nodded, startled back into the present.

"I'm Juan-Carlos," he said briskly, extending his hand. "The Triumvirate are expecting you. Follow me, please."

The Triumvirate? Will thought, feeling his lips automatically slide into a half smile. That was definitely a unique way to describe the owners of the elite security company. And the hint of droll humor he'd heard behind the description was especially puzzling.

Juan-Carlos led him down a carpeted hall, past several offices into a large lounge area that looked more like a man cave than any sort of business room. A flat-screen television was anchored to the wall—currently tuned to a Braves baseball game—and a well-used pool table overlooked downtown proper. A stainless-steel refrigerator—no doubt stocked with the drinks and snacks the three of them were currently enjoying—stood against another wall. Various bits of technology—laptops, cell phones, MP3 players and the like—lay scattered over the battered coffee table, along with their feet.

Seated on dark leather furniture, the three men stood when he entered. Brian Payne was easily recognizable with his blond hair and penetrating ice-blue eyes. Nicknamed the Specialist, Payne was notorious for his ability to always do things right the first time. Much like failure, half-assed wasn't an option.

Equally impressive with his supposed genius-level IQ, Jamie Flanagan had dark curls that gave him a boyish quality, but the set of his shoulders and the line of his jaw let a man know that the Irish-American former soldier was a force to be reckoned with.

Guy McCann rounded out the rest of the Triumvirate, with a reputation of recklessness and luck that bordered on the providential. McCann's smile was a little irreverent, but the shrewd green gaze currently sizing him up felt anything but flippant.

It was Payne who spoke first. "Forrester," he said, striding forward to shake Will's hand. "Welcome to Ranger Security."

Flanagan grinned, plopped back onto the couch and shoved a potato chip into his mouth. "The perks kick ass."

"Ignore him," McCann piped up, snatching the remote control out of Jamie's reach. "We do actually work," he drawled.

"On occasion" came the long-suffering voice of Juan-Carlos as he quietly shut the door.

Guy glared at Payne. "He's getting a little too mouthy for a secretary."

"He's an office manager," Payne corrected. "And he's indispensable. Which he knows."

"If he continues to smirk at me, what's not going to be indispensable are his teeth," Guy threatened. "He's a subordinate. He should act like it."

Will wondered if they knew he referred to the three of them as the Triumvirate, but decided not to mention it. He didn't want Juan-Carlos to lose any of those pricey porcelain veneers on his account.

"Can I get you something to drink?" Payne offered, jerking a thumb toward the refrigerator.

Will shook his head. "I'm good, thanks."

"Have a seat," Jamie told him, gesturing toward one of the empty chairs. "We're pretty informal around here."

He actually liked that, Will thought. These guys were obviously just as comfortable in their own skin as they were with one another. It was the sort of familiarity that took countless hours and inherent trust and he instinctively found himself wanting to be a part of it. To share in the easy camaraderie. Though he'd been happy about the job—about having an alternative at all to the military career he'd envisioned—for the first time since he'd officially walked off base, Will instinctively knew he'd found where he belonged.

This was going to work. He felt it.

"How's my grandfather-in-law?" Flanagan wanted to know.

Will smiled and tried to frame a diplomatic response. Colonel Carl Garrett was an old warhorse with a piss-and-gravel voice that had been honed on the battlefield and fired in the boardroom. Will had a lot of respect for the man, but he'd ruffled more than a few feathers through the years. Of course, no one could be in the colonel's position without pissing off a lot of other people. It was the nature of the career.

"Well," Will finally managed. He waited a beat. "The same as always."

"So he's still an interfering, egotistical old bastard on a power trip, then?" McCann said. He snorted. "Figures."

Payne laughed. "Careful, Guy. That interfering, egotistical old bastard is responsible for some of our best help—" his cool gaze slid to Will "—and our newest recruit." He lifted a brow. "You've reviewed the employment package?"

He had and was still astonished. "It's generous."

And that was putting it lightly. In addition to the salary, the benefits were beyond amazing. Preferring that specialists lived in close proximity, Payne had purchased the entire building and renovated the upper floors into apartments. Though Jamie and Guy lived in Atlanta only part-time, Payne was in residence at all times in the penthouse suite. Considering he'd been in the service since college, Will had little in the way of personal belongings and even less in the home furnishing department. That he would be able to move right into an outfitted apartment was a perk he could genuinely appreciate.

"You'll earn it," Payne assured him. He handed him a laptop, a cell phone and a Glock 9 mm. "Tools of the trade. All of the software you'll need to interface with our programs here at the office have already been loaded onto the computer. Numbers are programmed into the phone and your permit to carry concealed is in the laptop bag." He shrugged. "Doubt you'll need a weapon for this first case, but better armed than not, in my opinion."

He wouldn't need a weapon for his first case? What exactly did that mean? Will wondered.

"Do you need a car?" Payne asked. "I've got a couple in the garage."

Will shook his head. He'd actually just traded in his old Jeep Wrangler for a new Black Rubicon.

"Here are the keys to your apartment," Payne said, tossing them lightly to him. He released a small breath. "That covers everything but the briefing on your first assignment."

McCann slid a folder across the coffee table to him. "It's a bit unusual," he said, and the small smile playing over his lips did little to inspire confidence.

Will flipped open the file and quickly scanned the first page. Theodore Watson, seventy-six, missing from his home for the past few days. He read on and immediately understood McCann's grin.

"A treasure hunt?" he asked dubiously, glancing up at Payne.

Jamie chuckled. "In a manner of speaking. Mr. Watson is looking for his great-great-grandfather's treasure. According to his family history, this particular grandfather had amassed quite a fortune in jewels. Afraid that the Union troops were going to seize his possessions, like many other people who lived in the South who had any wealth, he hid them. Unfortunately, he died before he recovered them from his hiding place and hadn't shared their whereabouts with anyone else."

"Or he could have, and that lucky soul kept it for himself," McCann pointed out. "The Watsons are practically royalty in the small burg of Begonia, Georgia. They're old money. Lots of land."

Will frowned. "So it's his family who've hired us? Is Mr. Watson a danger to himself? Got any health issues that make his disappearance particularly disturbing?" Granted the man wasn't exactly a spring chicken, but from the looks of this file he lived by himself, which would indicate that he was relatively healthy, at any rate.

Payne, McCann and Flanagan shared a look. "Tad Watson, Theo's son, is more concerned with keeping up appearances than his father's actual safety," McCann explained with a twisted smile. "From what we've been able to discern, Theo has been looking for this treasure for more than sixty years, and is a bit on the eccentric side. Tad doesn't approve."

"He's an embarrassment," Jamie said, pulling a shrug. "Tad wants him found so that he can do damage control."

"He's throwing around words like *senile* and *dementia* and *diminished capacity,*" Payne said. "Laying the groundwork to have him committed, or at the very least put into an assisted-living facility."

Though he'd never met Theodore Watson in his life, Will found himself inexplicably annoyed on his behalf. What the hell was wrong with people? he wondered. Whatever happened to respecting your elders? Furthermore, this was the South. Eccentricities were typically celebrated. Crazy, so long as it wasn't harmful, was charming down here.

"The senior Watson is much more philanthropic than his son would like him to be," Jamie added with a grimace. "If he managed to put his father into a home, he'd be able to control the family finances."

In other words, he was greedy. Impossibly, Will liked Tad even less.

"At any rate, the son has provided us with a list of probable locations his father could be," Payne announced after a significant pause.

"He hasn't looked himself?" Will asked, surprised.

Another uncomfortable look. "Tad is actually out of the country."

"Flying over the Atlantic right about now, wouldn't you say, Jamie?" McCann remarked. He tossed a handful of M&M's down his throat.

Atlantic? Right now? Will frowned. "Let me get this straight. His father is missing, so he's concerned enough to hire one of the premier security firms in the country...but he's *not* concerned enough to postpone a business trip?"

"Actually, it's a vacation," Payne corrected, his voice chilly. "Italy. He'll be checking in periodically and wants to be notified as soon as his father is located."

How considerate, Will thought, utterly disgusted. He grimaced. "Right."

"There's also a list of acquaintances in there, people he might have contacted before he left," Jamie said.

Will looked up. "He didn't mention he was leaving to his son?"

McCann snorted. "I sure as hell wouldn't, if I was the old guy, would you?"

He supposed not. Still…

"We know this isn't exactly an exciting or glamorous first assignment, but it's what pays the bills," Payne said.

He didn't give a damn about exciting or glamorous, and after a minute he confided as much. "I'm just…thankful to have a job, to have a place here. It's more than I could have hoped for, particularly considering I made the decision to leave abruptly."

Payne's calm gaze found his. "We know exactly what that's like. It's why we're here, you know."

And he did know. Garrett had given him the abbreviated reason as to why Payne, McCann and Flanagan had left the military. They'd lost a dear friend and comrade, Danny Levinson, and each of them felt as if they were in part to blame. Couldn't be any easier to live with that than what he was currently struggling with, Will thought.

Help me, he heard again, for what felt like the

thousandth time. The tiny, faltering voice. Fearful yet trusting and so, so weak...

"It gets easier," Jamie said, his eyes grave with understanding.

Will merely shrugged, hoping like hell that was true. It sure couldn't get any worse.

"THIS ONE IS STAYING," McCann announced as soon as Will Forrester disappeared around the door frame.

"Ordinarily when you make predictions like that, I think you're completely full of shit, Guy, but in this instance I think you might be right," Jamie agreed.

Brian Payne silently concurred. Though they'd lost their past two employees to other career paths—and women—Forrester seemed different. There was a sadness, an ownership to Will's grief that he recognized, as well. Hell, who was he kidding? They could all identify. Innocent blood on your hands was something they could all empathize with. Though Payne had realized that it wasn't completely his fault that Danny had died, there was a part of him that would always feel responsible for his death all the same. Like Will, it didn't matter that the intel was faulty, that he'd done everything he was supposed to do.

He'd lost a man.

And Will Forrester, according to Garrett, had had a child die in his arms.

Terrible stuff, that.

"What do you think?" Jamie asked. "You think he's going to have any trouble making the transition to our way of life?"

Payne shook his head. "Not at all. You've read everything I've read. He knows what he's doing. Was one hell of a soldier who simply lost the stomach for war."

"With good reason," McCann said. "Damn, how do you find your happy place after something like that? How do you move forward?"

Jamie passed a hand over his face. "I don't know. Women and children, you know? That's the stuff of nightmares."

Though Garrett had been very vague with the details of Forrester's last mission, Payne knew that it had involved the accidental death of innocent civilians. Payne had willingly fought terrorists without batting a lash because he'd been fighting for the greater good against an enemy who wasn't above killing innocent women and children. Conscienceless zealots bent on revenge and power. But if he was ever involved in a mission like Forrester's, which had resulted in the death of those they were trying to protect… He didn't know how he would cope and, frankly, was thankful that he'd never have to try.

"I liked him," Jamie said. "My gut says he's a good guy."

"If we're going to start talking about feelings, then I'm outta here," McCann said, purposely lightening the moment.

"Kiss my ass, Guy," Jamie told him, hurling an empty plastic soda bottle at his head. "You know what I mean."

"Do you think we should have mentioned the chick?" Guy asked, shooting Payne a look.

The chick in question was Rhiannon Palmer—good friend to Theo—who was hell-bent on finding him, as well. Having been told by Tad—her ex-boyfriend—that Ranger Security was on the case, Rhiannon had already been in contact many times asking for updates. A local elementary guidance counselor specializing in emotional intelligence, she was pushy, feisty and had all the tenacity of a bulldog.

"She's on the list of acquaintances," Payne said, and smiled.

And she was now Will Forrester's problem.

2

RHIANNON PALMER GLARED ominously down at her cell phone as she absorbed the last text message from her miserable, sanctimonious ex-boyfriend and felt a low growl build in the back of her throat.

Butt out. It's under control.

She fired off a final go-to-hell message, then sank back against the cushions of her porch swing and tried to plan her next move. Her dog, an Australian shepherd named Keno, determinedly nosed her palm and Rhiannon gave her an absentminded rub.

"Oh, Theo," she moaned aloud. "Where the hell are you?"

Honestly, if she hadn't been so worried about

her dear friend and mentor, she could quite happily have throttled him. He'd purposely waited to make his escape while she'd been finishing up the final class in emotional intelligence, a course she taught at the local community college during the summer. August through May, she was the guidance counselor at Begonia Elementary School, a job she genuinely loved.

Rhiannon could perfectly identify with so many of the kids who walked through her door. She'd been the shy, insecure little bookworm with the added freakishness of being able to accurately read people's moods. Hidden things, even, which weren't readily discernible on the surface.

With the exception of Elizabeth Alston, her best friend, it had made her an outcast on the playground, and had made adults a little too uncomfortable around her. Of course, having a child pick up on your secret crush on the assistant principal—particularly when you were married to the basketball coach—couldn't have been easy, Rhiannon thought, remembering that particular incident with a small smile.

At any rate, it wasn't until she'd met Theodore Watson, a local librarian with plenty of money and too much time on his hands, that Rhiannon had been made by an adult to feel anything other than odd. Even her parents, bless their hearts, hadn't been quite sure what to make of their daughter, a fact that she'd been aware of from the time she was a toddler.

But Theo... Theo had made her feel *special*. He'd looked at her and seen potential, and she'd loved him ever since.

As a semi-empath himself and possessing a keen interest in emotional intelligence—or EI—Theo recognized her unique ability and had quickly made her feel more at home in her own mind than she'd ever been in her life. Not only had he helped her hone her skill at recognizing others' emotions, but he'd taught her how to use her own to influence the people around her. Despite her admittedly hot temper, Rhiannon could be quite soothing when she wanted to be. She glared at her phone again.

Right now she wasn't in the mood to soothe anyone, even herself. She was enjoying her irritation.

Stupid Tad, she thought. Moron. Idiot. Gigantic ass.

Though she'd dated Tad only to make Theo happy, Rhiannon nevertheless bitterly regretted the decision. It had taken less than a minute into their first meeting for her to realize that a love match wasn't in their future, but Theo had been so happy—so overjoyed that Tad had asked her out—she hadn't been able to refuse.

Unfortunately, much like the first date, the relationship had quickly ended in disaster. Though she'd been ready to pull the plug from the get-go, Tad had beaten her to the punch, evidently sensing her uninterest, and had dumped her publicly on Facebook.

Mortified didn't begin to cover it.

In addition to dumping her, he'd complained loudly to anyone who would listen in their small town about how "clingy" and "needy" she was, which was absolute bullshit. Rhiannon was many things, but clingy and needy weren't among them. Thankfully most people were well aware of her true character and Tad's penchant for self-importance, but it hadn't lessened her irritation or humiliation all that much.

Furthermore, that had been three years ago and Tad still had the audacity to act as if she was stalking him and couldn't get over him.

She couldn't get over him because she'd never been *on* him to start with. There was nothing to get over. She saw Tad only when she absolutely couldn't avoid him.

Unfortunately, no matter how much it irritated her to have to be in contact with him, Rhiannon didn't see any other choice. Tad had taken off for his Italian vacation, certain that his father had merely gone off on another relatively harmless search for the Watson treasure. He was embarrassed by his father's continued obsession with what he thought was a "ridiculous old story manufactured after one too many shots of moonshine."

Rhiannon didn't agree with Tad in the least and trusted Theo's instincts. He was a brilliant man who wouldn't have wasted sixty years of his life looking for something if he hadn't genuinely believed it was there. Because his family had wearied of listening to him go on and on about the family jewels, they'd actually talked at length about it many times.

If the jewels were real—and she, too, suspected they were—then she knew beyond a shadow of doubt that Theo would eventually find them. He'd actually called and left her a message the day he'd left.

"Rhi, I think I've got it!" he'd crowed. "Matthew 6:21. 'For where your treasure is, your heart will be also.' Don't you see? I've been looking in the wrong place. All this time and it's been right under my nose. Don't worry, dear. I'll be in touch."

But he'd been gone three days—plenty long enough for him to have found what he thought he was going to find if it had been where he thought it was and…nothing. Ordinarily, Rhiannon wouldn't have been worried. Theo was a youthful seventy-six, fit and relatively healthy.

But recently Theo had been diagnosed with

diabetes and, just like a typical man, he wasn't taking it seriously enough. He didn't monitor his blood sugar the way he should and routinely got too caught up in his research to eat regularly. Skipping meals in any circumstance wasn't healthy, but was particularly harmful for diabetics.

Theo had made her—and his physician—promise not to tell Tad. Due to his father's notoriously generous philanthropy, it was no secret that Tad was just looking for an excuse to move him into an assisted-living home and attempt to garner power of attorney over him. Furthermore, Tad and his father had different dreams for Watson Plantation, ones they'd been having increasingly frequent arguments about.

The Watson Plantation was unique in the fact that the family had never sold a single inch of land from the original plot. It was eighteen hundred acres of rich soil, and Watsons had been farming it for almost two hundred years. Through Theo, Rhiannon knew that they rotated the crops to keep the earth in good condition. She loved it most when they planted cotton, seeing that sea of fluffy white bolls nodding in the breeze.

True to his heritage, Theo was determined to keep farming the land and keep the old home place in the family, to preserve it for future generations of Watsons.

Tad had visions of trendy subdivisions, strip malls and fast-food restaurants. Or more accurately, the money that would be garnered as a result of selling off each bit of the estate acre by profitable acre. As an only child, Tad had no interest in maintaining the family legacy. He just wanted to line his pockets and travel the world, preferably with a supermodel at his side. He had no time and even less respect for his father, which annoyed the sheer hell out of Rhiannon.

Rather than skip his vacation and look for his father himself, Tad had hired a security company out of Atlanta to do the job. Though it had taken quite a bit of swearing, Rhiannon had finally managed to get the name of the company out of him and had called them many times over the past twenty-four hours. According to Brian Payne, the gentleman she'd been speaking with, their operative would be in town and on the case today and, being as close to Theo as anyone else, she fully expected a visit.

And then she would make sure she got to tag along, because there was no way she could continue to sit here and do nothing. Though taking off on her own had occurred to her, the agency's resources were better and more advanced than hers. They could track phone calls, credit cards and the like. If she had a general idea which way he had headed, Rhiannon thought Theo had given her enough information over the past several years to figure out exactly where he was going.

And the sooner she found him, the better. Considering the diabetes and his poor attitude about it, she wasn't going to be able to take an easy breath until then.

She might as well be breathing where it would do her some good.

Or she could not breathe at all, Rhiannon thought as the best-looking man she'd ever seen in her life suddenly loped up her sidewalk.

Sweet God.

She almost swooned.

Every bit of the moisture in her mouth promptly evaporated and the tops of her thighs tingled with heat that had absolutely nothing to do with the mid-morning sun. A line of gooseflesh marched up her spine and camped in the back of her neck, making her entire scalp prickle with awareness. A violent full-body blush stained her skin from one end to the other and, though she knew it was simply her imagination, she could have sworn she heard the faintest strands of porn music as he stepped fully into view.

Six and a half feet of rock-hard, splendidly proportioned muscle and bone stood in an open-legged stance in front of her, showcasing long, lean legs and a crotch that instantly captured her gaze.

Probably because she was practically at eye level with it, Rhiannon thought faintly.

He wore a black T-shirt that hugged every rippling muscle and a pair of trendy sunglasses she instantly wished he'd remove. Confidence straightened his shoulders and shadowed the angular curve of his jaw, and a small cleft she had the almost irrepressible urge to lick bisected his chin. His hair was a golden-brown and shorn into a military cut that made him look all the more like a badass.

His mouth, possibly the most sensual thing she'd ever had the pleasure to gaze upon, shifted into a smile, and the simple rearrangement of his lips made something in her middle go all warm and squishy.

Hell, even her dog was panting.

He removed his glasses, revealing a pair of eyes that were a pale misty gray—almost disconcertingly clear—and lined with sinfully thick dark brown lashes.

He was sex incarnate, Rhiannon thought.

And she instinctively knew she was in trouble.

"Rhiannon Palmer?" he asked, his voice a husky baritone that put her in mind of rumpled sheets and massage oil. She tested the mood around him, and several things hit her at once—interest (gratifying, of course), confidence (also attractive—he knew what he was doing) and a sadness so deep and profound she almost gasped when she felt it. A frown worked its way across her brow. *Loss, regret, shame.* She could feel them all now. A tangled mess of remorse and misery so heavy she was surprised he could walk beneath its burden.

Denial was a powerful thing, though.

Rhiannon stood on wobbly legs and struggled to find her focus. "You've found her."

He smiled again. "I'm Will Forrester with Ranger Security and I'd like to talk to you about Theo Watson."

She'd thought as much. "Ah." She sighed. "I've been expecting you."

He blinked. "You have?"

"I've been speaking with your associate," she explained. "Brian Payne."

"Right," he said, though something in his gaze shifted. Irritation, perhaps? Intriguing. "Do you mind if I ask you a few questions about Mr. Watson?"

"Only if you don't mind if we go into the house," she said, ducking around him to get the front door. "It's getting a little hot out here."

And with him tagging along, she didn't think she was going to get any cooler, but she thought she'd fare better with the benefit of climate control. Honestly, she'd never had such a visceral reaction to a man before. It was as terrifying as it was thrilling. She tried to tell herself that she'd simply been too long without sex—more than a year, shamefully—but knew better.

It was him. Every beautifully proportioned inch of him.

"Sure," he said, left essentially without a choice.

She clicked her tongue for the dog and watched the shaggy creature promptly go and sprawl across one of the air-conditioning vents.

Having seen Keno's antics, as well, Will Forrester chuckled. The sound seemed rusty, which she found unaccountably sad. This was a guy who should laugh. "Smart dog."

"Too smart," Rhiannon agreed. "She can open the refrigerator, too."

He shot her an impressed, slightly disbelieving look. "Seriously?"

Rhiannon nodded once. "Seriously. She knows better than to take anything out, of course, but has to do it a couple of times a day just to let me know that she can." She gestured toward the couch. "Have a seat, please. Can I get you something to drink? I'm going to have a glass of tea, so…"

He nodded his thanks. "In that case, yes."

Rhiannon made her way to the kitchen, which was open to her living-room, dining-room combo. "Lemon?"

"Sure."

While she fixed the drinks, she watched him covertly. His keen gaze quickly noted everything in the room, from the pictures on her mantel to the slightly crooked throw rug in front of her couch.

He straightened it, and in that lone, impulsive gesture, she was able to size him up.

Will Forrester liked to be in control.

Pondering that, she felt a small smile slide over her lips as she returned to the living room. "Here you go," she said, handing him the glass.

He accepted with a grateful smile and took a sip, then sighed. "Thank you. That hits the spot."

One of them at least, Rhiannon thought, suppressing a laugh. Good Lord, had she ever seen a more beautiful man? Had she ever gazed at such masculine perfection in her life? He was criminally handsome. Even his ears were sexy. They had to be; otherwise she wouldn't be fantasizing about breathing into one of them right now.

He stared at her and a small grin played over his lips, as though he knew exactly what she was thinking. Impossible, she thought, and resisted the urge to press the glass to her forehead.

She took a chair opposite him. "So how is the investigation going so far?" she asked. "Have you had any leads?"

He winced. "Not exactly. I've been making calls during the drive over and so far I haven't found so much as a trace of him. He used his credit card to fill up with gas at Big Bo's Gas Mart on Friday, withdrew a sizable amount of cash from the local ATM and has completely fallen off radar."

Rhiannon grimaced. He must have known that Tad would hire someone to find him, she thought. Otherwise, why bother with using cash? "When you say a sizable amount of cash, just exactly how much are we talking about here?"

"Two thousand dollars."

"Eek," she said. "That'll buy a lot of gas, greasy food and cheap motel rooms, won't it?"

"If he's careful, a week to ten days," Will confirmed. "Do you have any idea where he might have gone?"

"He's looking for the treasure, obviously," she said, then shook her head. "The Watsons are originally from Philadelphia and they slowly migrated to the south, but that leaves a lot of territory, doesn't it?"

He nodded, jotting down a note in a small book. "It does…and it looks like it's my job to cover it. That's a start, at any rate." He stood and handed her his empty glass. "Thank you," he said. "I appreciate—"

Startled, Rhiannon stood, too. "You mean, you're leaving now? Right this second? For Philadelphia?"

He paused, and those shrewd gray eyes caught and held hers. She repressed a shiver. "I'm going to talk with a few other people in town first—friends, coworkers, the staff at the Watson Plantation—but if nothing comes of any of that, then yes, I'll be leaving shortly."

Good thing she'd already packed, then, Rhiannon thought. She'd actually thought they'd do a bit more poking around in town first, but this guy was obviously quite efficient. She'd been right not to strike out on her own. This would go a whole lot faster and a whole lot easier if they combined forces. The sooner she could make sure that Theo was okay—that he hadn't passed out from low blood sugar and tumbled down a stairwell or Lord knew what else—the better she'd feel.

That was her top priority at the moment, her only concern.

And then once she found out he was okay, she was going to verbally abuse him until he wished he hadn't been found. Damn him for making her worry like this. Didn't he know how important he was to her? Hadn't he known she'd be a wreck? Particularly given the diabetes? Couldn't he have invited her along, or at the very least let her know exactly where he was going?

She wasn't Tad, dammit.

More determined than ever, Rhiannon nodded once. "Okay," she said briskly. "Let me get my bag."

3

HER BAG? What the fu—

Before he could form the question, the beautiful—and evidently demented—creature darted from the living room and down a hall. Her bare feet slapped against the hardwood as she made her hasty retreat, bringing to his attention her curiously painted toes—hot-pink with silver stars.

No two ways about it. Rhiannon Palmer was quite possibly the sexiest woman he'd ever met in the flesh, or seen between the pages of a magazine, for that matter. She had long black hair that fell in wavy disarray around her elfin face, wide violet eyes and a mouth that put him in mind of sex. Though she wasn't what one could call classically beautiful, she had a memorable, unique face. That visage paired with an especially soft, curvy body and an ass that was ripe and lush sent her sexy quotient through the roof.

He'd taken one look at her and gone uncomfortably hard.

While he had to admit that wasn't a first, it was the first time since he'd left puberty behind.

Had he met her in any other circumstance, he would have been all over her like white on rice. He would have made a play for her faster than she could say *condom*.

Unfortunately, charming and witty aside, she didn't appear to be dealing with a full deck, and that point was never driven home more clearly than in that instant, when she strolled back into the living room with a rolling suitcase at her side. She'd put a pair of enormous sunglasses on her head and sparkly flip-flops on her feet and a bag big enough to house China over her shoulder.

"I'm ready," she announced, as if he should have been expecting this.

Will blinked. "Ready for what?"

"To go with you, of course."

He laughed uncomfortably and looked away before finding her gaze once more. "Er...that's really not necessary. I'm perfectly capable of—"

"I know that it's not necessary," she said. "It's expedient. You and I both have the same goal—to find Theo. It'll go quicker if we help each other."

He hated to point out the obvious, but... "I don't need your help."

Nor did he want it. In the first place, she was obviously...different. The word seemed a lot more charitable than *crazy*. In the second place, this was his first assignment for his new job and he'd just as soon not be distracted. In the third place, she was too damned sexy for his own good. And in the fourth place—damn, this was a long list—she unnerved him.

Will didn't like being unnerved.

Her laugh tinkled between them, and that sexy sound settled around his loins. "Yes, you do need me. You just don't know it yet."

Definitely crazy, Will thought. More's the pity. "In that case, I'll call you if I need your assistance." He smiled reassuringly and backed toward the door. "Don't worry. I'll find him."

Her smile turned a bit hard and she expelled a patient breath, as though he were the one being unreasonable. "Look, Mr. Forrester, you seem like a smart man, so I hope that this doesn't sound too patronizing, but...you don't know who you're looking for, and I do. Theo has been over every aspect of the Watson treasure story with me backward and forward. It's quite possible that you'll stumble upon a lead and not even realize it."

Will paused, looking for a flaw in her logic. He

supposed even sexy, crazy people had moments of lucidity. "True," he admitted. "But if that's the case, then why haven't you been out looking for him?"

"I have looked around here, in all the usual places," she said. "But he's not in town. If he was, I'd have found him by now. Furthermore, if he was staying close to home, he wouldn't have needed the cash—that says road trip to me—and he wouldn't have left me a message telling me not to worry."

Will's senses went on point and he felt his gaze narrow. "He left you a message? When? Do you still have it?" He wasn't aware of any contact with anyone after Watson supposedly disappeared.

"Of course," she said. She walked over to her answering machine. "He left it three days ago. That's the last I heard from him." She pressed the play button.

"Rhiannon, Tad here. Please stop harassing the Ranger Security people. Finding Dad isn't going to score you any points with me—"

She flushed and skipped over the message to the next.

Ah, Will thought. So that was her game, eh? From the sounds of things she and Tad had had a falling-out and Rhiannon was interested in helping find Theo Watson in order to put herself back in his good graces. He found himself unreasonably disappointed.

"Ignore him," she said, her voice throbbing with anger. "He's an ass."

Sour grapes, then? Had Tad taken a woman with him to Italy? Will wondered. His initial impression of Tad painted the man as a selfish, disrespectful boor. Crazy or not, he would have figured she'd have better taste. The thought made him slightly nauseated.

"Rhi, I think I've got it!" an older male voice said over the machine. "Matthew 6:21. 'For where your treasure is, your heart will be also.' Don't you see? I've been looking in the wrong place. All this time and it's been right under my nose. Don't worry, dear. I'll be in touch."

Excitement and affection rang in every syllable in Theo's voice and it was quite obvious that he adored Rhiannon Palmer. The fact that he would leave her a message advising her not to worry, but didn't bestow the same courtesy on his son told Will that he either didn't care whether Tad worried or not, or didn't expect him to be concerned in the first place. And considering that Tad was in Italy and Rhiannon was here, determined to go with him to help find Watson...

Well, clearly the older man was an excellent judge of character.

Nevertheless, it didn't change the fact that she couldn't tag along with him. Granted, he was new to the security business, but he didn't think that was proper protocol at all. After more than a decade of following orders and procedures, Will had learned to appreciate not only the chain of command, but the boundaries it put into place.

She was over the line.

"Does Tad know about this message?" Will asked. "He didn't mention it."

She lifted her chin. "No, I didn't tell Tad. He thinks his father is a ridiculous old fool and has evidenced his true concern by not changing his vacation plans." She crossed her arms over her chest. "I don't owe Tad anything. Furthermore, if Theo had wanted to call him, he could have."

"True." He considered her thoughtfully and finally asked the question that was driving him nuts. Ridiculous. He ought not even care. It didn't matter. And yet… "So you and Tad are a thing?"

She snorted and rolled her eyes. "I went out with Tad because Theo had grand dreams of me being able to turn his spoiled, shallow son into some sort of a redeemable facsimile of a man. The minute Tad realized that I was not going to fall into bed with him, he dumped me—via Facebook—and has continued with the false delusion that my greatest desire is our reconciliation." Her brows formed a straight line. *"It is not."* Her expression softened with genuine affection. "I do, however, utterly adore his father—he's been a better father to me than my own—and I am desperately worried about him."

Maybe she wasn't on medication after all, Will decided. Maybe she was just a little odd. Charmingly so, he had to confess. Charming + sexy = Trouble, he thought, tearing his gaze away from her ripe mouth. Another thought struck.

"My information says he's of sound mind and in good health. Is that wrong?"

She hesitated long enough for him to notice. "It is."

He waited. "But…" he prodded.

Her shrewd gaze probed his, evidently deliberating how to answer him. "Are you obligated to pass along any information I give you to Tad?"

A warning bell went off in his head. She was hiding something from him. Something that he instinctively knew was crucial to his case. "That would be at my discretion, of course."

She winced, disappointed. "That's not the answer I was hoping for."

Will leveled a gaze at her. "If there are extenuating circumstances that I am not aware of regarding Mr. Watson, then I would urge you to tell me."

"Only if I can trust you not to mention this to Tad. The last thing he needs is more ammunition to try and put his father into a home." An ominous expression settled over her face, putting him in mind of an angry kitten. "I won't give it to him."

Senile and *dementia* and *diminished capacity,* Will thought, Payne's words coming back to him.

"He's fine, really," she said. "He's just…" She trailed off, seemingly unwilling to finish.

"I will not mention this to Tad," Will said, hoping he wasn't going to regret making that rash promise. For reasons that eluded him, he wanted her to confide in him.

She melted, and the relieved smile that slid over her lips made him feel as if he'd just battled a dragon on her behalf. "He's recently been diagnosed with diabetes and isn't taking it seriously," she confessed. "He's prone to skip meals and not check his sugar. It makes me a nervous wreck," she said, her brow clouding with concern. "Obviously he doesn't want Tad to know. It would just be one more reason to try and get him into a home where he could be 'properly looked after.'" Bitter sarcasm coated her last words.

Will frowned. This changed things. His grandmother—he made a mental note to call her later—was diabetic and Will knew firsthand how quickly things could go south with the illness. He'd had to get her a hard candy or a quick glass of orange juice more times than he cared to count.

She bit her bottom lip. "I'm sure he's probably fine, but knowing that he could let his sugar drop too low, that he could fall or get hurt and not knowing where he is…" She made a low, frustrated noise in her throat. "It's driving me crazy. I could throttle him, truly. So you see, that's why I have to go. I can't just stay here. I *can* help you. I know you don't think so right now—I can tell," she added with a small knowing smile that completely unnerved him. "But I can."

While he understood her concern and knew it was genuine, Will shook his head, albeit more reluctantly. He was relatively certain taking her along was against company policy, and even if it wasn't, it would be better for his sanity if she remained here. She was too damned tempting and, though he'd always prided himself on his self-control, there was no point in putting himself through hell to hang on to it. "Ms. Palmer—"

"Rhiannon, please."

"Rhiannon, I'm going to level with you. This is my first assignment for Ranger Security—"

Her eyes widened. "Then you definitely don't want to screw it up."

"*And* I really don't want to risk it by allowing you to accompany me. I'm sure you understand." *You also scare the hell out of me,* he silently added. *And it's been too long since I've properly bedded a woman and you are too tempting by half.* Note to self—get laid ASAP *after* this assignment.

She drew back and leveled a long look at him, one that felt as if she was probing the hidden recesses of his mind. It made him distinctly uncomfortable.

Finally she released a fatalistic sigh. "The hard way, then?" She nodded once, as though agreeing with herself. "Fine."

Charmingly unhinged, Will thought again.

But he'd won.

For the moment, anyway.

SHE SHOULD HAVE BEEN a private investigator, Rhiannon thought as she watched Will Forrester disappear into the bank. This "tailing" thing was ridiculously easy. And he'd even gotten a head start. She'd had to make sure Keno had enough food and water until Elizabeth came by to pick her up, lock up the house and load her things into the car.

Of course, she'd imagined that he'd go straight to the Watson Plantation and she'd been right. She'd merely waited for him to come out—twinkling her fingers at his astonished face as he'd made his way back to his car—then followed him here. She glanced at the clock and winced when her stomach growled. One o'clock. She hoped he got hungry soon. She could use a bit of lunch, and the special today at Willie's Diner was meat loaf—her favorite.

In the meantime she decided to give Elizabeth a try again. Her friend was a gymnastics instructor, and the only time she could catch her during the day was between classes. Thankfully, this was one of those times.

"Twinkle Toes," Elizabeth answered. The sound of rowdy children and dance music bled through the line.

Rhiannon dug through her purse until she found a granola bar. "Hey, it's me." She tore into the packet with her teeth.

"I saw where you'd called earlier. Sorry I missed you. Any news on Theo?"

"A little," Rhiannon told her, and relayed the information she'd gotten from Will. "He's definitely on the move. The eternal question, of course, is to where?"

"You would know better than anyone else," Liz said.

Rhiannon rolled her eyes. "Why don't you tell that to Mr. Security Expert? He wasn't exactly receptive to my join-forces plan."

She chuckled. "He's a man. Did you really expect him to be?"

"I expected him to be logical."

"He's got a penis. He's incapable of being

logical." A bitter undertone colored her voice and Rhiannon instantly became annoyed on her friend's behalf.

Her lips twisted. "Speaking of dicks, any word from Mark?"

"Not one," Elizabeth replied.

She *tsked* sympathetically. "Sorry, Liz. He's a total idiot. You know that, right?"

She chuckled sadly. "True," she said. "But I was the bigger fool for ever falling for him to start with."

"Nah," Rhiannon said, though in truth she quite honestly had never understood Mark's appeal. He was relatively handsome, she supposed, but left a lot to be desired when it came to intelligence. Then again, though she was a bit of an expert when it came to emotions, Rhiannon had never fully understood love.

Of course, considering she'd never actually been in love, how could she possibly understand it?

To be completely honest, the emotion sort of terrified her. She'd seen people do strange things, completely lose their own identity, sacrifice their self-respect, their dignity over the puzzlingly powerful emotion. And the jealousy it inspired? Sweet hell, she never wanted to deal with that.

Her own parents had an extremely volatile relationship—screaming and crying one minute, kissing the next. It was a roller coaster of emotions that had completely drained her as a child and young adult...and she'd just been a bystander. She genuinely didn't know how they stood it. How they bore that kind of emotional upheaval all the time. And for what?

Love.

Well, no thank you, Rhiannon thought. She would pass. At least on romantic love. She had experienced the other sorts. The love of friendship, for instance. Like Elizabeth. Like Theo. And she loved her parents, as well, but there was a small part of her that was thankful they'd retired to Florida and taken their emotional maelstrom with them.

That was the problem with being an empath— she felt everything much more strongly. The good *and* the bad.

Though she knew Theo and Elizabeth worried about her, Rhiannon was quite content on her own. When she wanted sex, she had sex. She was choosy, of course, and didn't invite just any old guy into her body. But she always purposely chose men who were interested in the same thing she was—a brief physical relationship only. No strings, no expectations, no declarations of undying love.

That was precisely what she was trying to avoid.

Rhiannon was secure enough in her own skin and happy enough with her own company. Did she occasionally experience a pang of longing to be in love and loved in return? Yes. After she watched a romantic comedy or when she passed nuzzling couples on the street. But the sensation quickly passed, or it used to, rather.

Much as she loathed admitting it, those bouts of longing for a deeper connection to another person were growing more frequent of late. She wasn't exactly sure what was bringing on the desire and, while a big proponent of EI—which was, in part, learning to identify and deal with your emotions properly—Rhiannon found herself a little reluctant to tap too fully into that part of herself.

Will Forrester exited the bank, and his step faltered when he saw her car. His gaze tangled with hers and the strangest sensation fluttered through her middle—expectation, maybe? Desire, definitely. But something more. Something she couldn't readily identify, which was almost more disconcerting than the feeling itself.

"You're sure you don't mind keeping my dog for a few days?" Rhiannon asked Elizabeth distractedly, though she knew the answer.

"Not at all," she said. "I'll pick her up this afternoon when I leave the studio."

"Thanks, I appreciate it."

"So…if he won't let you come with him, then what exactly are you going to do?"

Rhiannon smiled as she watched him make his way to his car. She could feel his irritation rolling at her in annoyed waves of displeasure. "I'm following him. It's driving him nuts," she said cheerfully.

Elizabeth laughed. "What? How do you know?"

"Because he keeps glaring at me." She got the impression that Will Forrester was used to calling the shots and hated having his plans thwarted. She pegged him as a methodical list maker who balked at the idea of spontaneity. He was too regimented, too controlled, and she had the irrational urge to shake him up.

Liz chuckled again. "Intimidated?"

"Not in the least."

"I didn't think so. So tell me about this guy. I'm picturing Columbo. Short, stocky, bad suit, needs a shave."

Rhiannon's gaze lingered on Will's mouthwatering ass, and another grin slid over her lips. "Er… not exactly. Go look up tall, dark and handsome," she said. "His picture will be there."

"Oh, really?" Elizabeth replied, an ooo-la-la in her voice.

"Pure eye candy, Liz. Utterly gorgeous." And

that was putting it mildly. He was magnificently handsome, sinfully sexy. While she'd never been strictly in love, she'd been in lust a few times.

The tingly heat that had flooded her body the instant she'd laid eyes on Will Forrester was completely out of the realm of her experience. Even the bottoms of her feet had buzzed.

"Deets," Elizabeth demanded. "I need details. Hair?"

"Brown. Short. Classic military high and tight." Aha, Rhiannon thought. The hair, the demeanor, the attention to detail. He was probably former military. That sure as hell made sense. She could certainly see that in his character.

"Eyes?"

How to describe them? she wondered. "Pale gray, but not flat. More silver I would say."

"Ooh, those sound nice."

They were. And when he looked at her... Man, her insides turned to mush.

"Body?"

Rhiannon grinned. *"Amazing."*

Elizabeth chuckled. "Ass?"

"Mouthwatering."

"Poor you," her friend remarked with faux sympathy. "Having to follow that guy around."

Rhiannon sighed dramatically. "It's a tough job, but somebody's got to do it."

She cranked her car and slid out into traffic behind Will. Her cell suddenly beeped, indicating a call waiting. She frowned. "Hey, Liz, I'm getting another call."

"Keep me posted," her friend said.

Rhiannon hit the flash button. "Hello."

"How long are you going to keep this up?" he asked, glaring at her from his rearview mirror.

She smiled brightly. "How did you get my number?"

"Same way I got your address. From the agency's file. How long?" he growled. Strangely, that was a turn-on. She wondered if he made the same noise in bed.

"For as long as it takes. Indefinitely. Forever. Whichever comes first. Why? Am I starting to get on your nerves?"

"No."

"Liar." She laughed. "I can see you scowling from here."

"Shit," he muttered, but she saw him smile. And oh, that smile…

"All of this could be avoided if you would simply let me help you."

"What part of *no* don't you understand?"

"I understand the word," she said, relieved when he pulled up in front of the diner. "It's the reasoning I'm having trouble with."

He sighed. "You're going to drive me crazy, aren't you?"

She fluffed her hair in the rearview mirror. "Only until you see sense."

4

RHIANNON PALMER SLID into the booth across from him and blithely snagged a menu from behind the napkin holder. "I'm so glad you finally stopped for lunch. I was starving."

Will chewed the inside of his cheek, reluctantly admiring her tenacity while simultaneously annoyed beyond reason. "Glad I could accommodate you."

She perused the menu. "I'm used to eating on a schedule, you know. I get cranky when I get hungry."

He moved the salt and pepper shakers to the middle of the table and arranged his silverware. "You're diabetic, too?"

"No," she said, popping the menu back into its place. "School. I'm the guidance counselor at Begonia Elementary."

Will snorted. "Guidance counselor?"

She straightened and those violet eyes narrowed fractionally. "My profession amuses you?"

"No, but imagining you as a guidance counselor does."

"Why?"

"Because my guidance counselor was a soft-spoken, bun-wearing cat lover who gave out 'Kindness Pays' stickers and cherry suckers." He purposely let his gaze drift over her. "You don't exactly fit the stereotype." Furthermore, weren't guidance counselors supposed to be soothing?

Rhiannon Palmer was anything but.

She was a live wire. One touch and she would fry him senseless, render him unable to form complete sentences. She was a red-hot mess—and despite better sense and a relatively keen sense of self-preservation, he was utterly fascinated by her.

He did not have time to be fascinated by her.

New job—one she was seemingly determined to ruin for him—missing old man with diabetes; the list was endless.

Honestly, when she'd made the "hard way" comment, he'd had no idea what to expect. He'd actually thought she meant that *she* was going to have to do things the hard way. Like, by herself. It had never occurred to him that the unpredictable beauty would *follow* him.

But that was exactly what she'd been doing all afternoon. He'd come out of the Watson Plantation manor—gorgeous, but ultimately unhelpful—and there she'd been. Sitting in a little hybrid SUV sporting a bumper sticker that said, "Well-behaved women rarely make history." And she'd actually waved at him, as though this were completely normal. As if they were old friends.

Bizarre.

"Afternoon, Rhi," the tall, thin waitress said. "I was beginning to wonder if you were going to show up today."

Rhiannon sent Will a pointed glare. "Unexpected delay. Please tell me you put a plate back for me," she wheedled shamelessly.

The waitress smiled. "Of course."

Her face brightened. "You're a peach, Wanda. Thanks."

"Tea?"

She nodded once. "Yep."

Wanda's attention swung to him. "And what can I get for you, sir?"

"I'll just have what she's having."

Wanda made a moue of regret. "Sorry. We're out."

Rhiannon smiled at him and offered up a small shrug. "Sorry. Have the open-faced roast beef," she suggested. "It's excellent."

"What are you having?"

"Meat loaf."

Dammit, he loved meat loaf.

"We should have gotten here earlier," she said, seemingly sensing his irrational displeasure.

Feeling like a total idiot, Will purposely schooled his expression into one that didn't make him look like a moron and simply nodded. "The roast beef, then," he said.

She widened her eyes in exaggerated wonder after Wanda walked away, and looked out the window toward the street. "Looks like I'm not the only one who gets cranky when he gets hungry," she remarked in a significant voice.

"I'm not cranky," he said. "I'm annoyed. There's a difference."

Another fatalistic shrug, as though this was all his fault. "You wanted to do it the hard way."

Though there was absolutely nothing dirty about what she'd said, his imagination nevertheless immediately leaped in that direction, which only served to irritate him further. Actually, he'd rather not do it at all, but he couldn't say that to her without fear of innuendo.

Will rubbed the bridge of his nose. "Please tell me that you aren't going to do this—follow me— all the way to Philadelphia."

Her gaze sharpened. "So that's where we're headed?"

He swore and leaned back.

"Watch your language," a little old lady in the booth directly behind him snapped. "I've got my grandson over here."

Rhiannon snickered as Will flushed beet-red and turned to offer an awkward apology.

Bloody frickin' hell.

Wanda returned with their plates and he stared broodingly at her meat loaf. She speared a bite and popped it into her mouth, then sighed with pleasure. The way her lips closed around her fork was particularly sensual and it didn't take much to imagine her mouth around another, increasingly hard part of his anatomy. Sweat suddenly dampened his upper lip.

She was going to be the death of him.

"You can't keep following me," he said, gallingly hearing a note of desperation in his own voice.

"You're right. It would be better if we traveled together." She sipped her tea. "We should take my car, though. It uses less of the world's finite resources."

Will dredged his soul for another ounce of patience. "That's not what I meant, and you know it."

She took a deep breath and set her fork aside for

the moment. "What is it about me going with you *exactly* that you object to?"

He blinked. "What?"

"Why *exactly* would it be so terrible for me to help you?"

It was a good question, Will would admit, and he wished he had an equally good answer. In all fairness, if she were going to trail after him—and he knew she was—it did make more sense for them to travel together. She had more knowledge about his target than any other person, and particular intel on the so-called treasure Watson was after. Logically, it made sense.

But…

He drew back and lifted his shoulders in an unconcerned shrug. "I've already told you. This is a new job. My first case. I may be new to the agency, but I've read the handbook—"

She gave an it-figures eye roll, which—while irritating—he chose to ignore.

"And *you* are against the rules." Strictly speaking, that was a lie. The handbook hadn't covered how to avoid irritating women hell-bent on "helping" him. "I can't afford any distractions," he finished.

"I would *not* be a distraction. I would be helpful."

Helpful or not, she would still be a distraction. A

beautiful, sexy, charming distraction he didn't have time for. Ranger Security was paying him to find Theodore Watson, not for trying to seduce the old man's friend. And Will knew himself well enough to know that he wouldn't be able to resist her. It had been too damned long since he'd been with a woman and she was too tempting by half. Human nature. Sexual chemistry. He'd seen a flicker of awareness in her eyes, too. It didn't take a genius to see where this would ultimately lead.

Bed.

And as wonderful as that might be—and he instinctively knew she would quite literally rock his world—this was not the time or place for it.

Furthermore, there was something about her that made him slightly…uneasy, for lack of a better description. Interesting behavior aside, there was something almost compelling about her. He could feel her drawing him in, and he had the most irrational urge to confide in her. To simply blurt out the truth. To tell her he couldn't afford to fuck up this job, that it was the last damned thing holding him to a career he used to love. That tied him to a past that, despite years of good deeds, he could no longer be proud of.

It was tainted with death.

Help me…

She leaned forward, laid her hand over his and smiled softly. "Are you okay?"

Predictably, her touch sizzled through him, chasing the images away with the flame of instant desire.

Will essayed a smile and was surprised at how easily the lie rolled off his tongue. "Of course." He paused. "But you still can't come with me."

HE WAS SUCH A LIAR, Rhiannon thought, and she was more than prudently intrigued by whatever was haunting him. The pain she'd felt settle around him like a shadow was positively debilitating and yet he'd merely smiled and managed to shrug it off. Not completely, of course, and there would come a point when he would not be able to do it, but...

It was none of her business.

Seriously. None of her concern. He was here to find Theo and that was all.

Furthermore, she instinctively knew—and didn't need any sort of EI to know this—that he would not welcome any interference on her part. Denial was getting him through whatever horror was haunting his soul and it was not her place to point out that it was futile. That a reckoning would eventually come.

Even if she wanted to.

Even now she could feel herself leaning toward

him, trying to draw him in and thereby draw out whatever was hurting him. She'd always been an emotional magnet, had always felt compelled to help people process their feelings, but even Rhiannon acknowledged this was more potent than anything she'd ever experienced before. She'd been telling him repeatedly that she could help him, but only now realized the secondary truth in her own statement.

Whether he knew it or not, Will Forrester needed her.

Unfortunately, she could tell that he was still as hell-bent as ever that she not come along with him. She didn't have to be able to read his mood to know that. It was written in every line in his face—the implacable gaze, the hard angle of his jaw, the determined firmness of his distractingly sexy chin.

Perhaps a new tack was in order. "Okay, fine. You win."

He blinked at her seeming capitulation and his gaze grew suddenly suspicious. "What do you mean I win? I win what?"

"I won't ask to come with you again. I'll just follow you, if you don't mind." She sighed heavily and played her trump card. "I'll feel safer."

Total crock of bullshit. She'd driven across the country alone when she was eighteen for the hell of it. Because she'd wanted to see the Pacific Ocean. She'd spent three months backpacking across Europe, staying in hostels and the like. While she wasn't exactly fearless—spiders scared the hell out of her—she was no shrinking violet and never would be.

But if playing one got her what she wanted, then so be it.

"Safer?" he deadpanned. "How so?"

"Oh, you know. A woman traveling alone. Without protection. Easy target for serial killers and rapists."

He snorted. "I think you are perfectly capable of taking care of yourself."

She inwardly preened at the comment, but purposely furrowed her brow. "I hope so," she said. "I've got some mace." And a taser and a brown belt, but he didn't need to know that.

His cheek creased with a smile and he leaned back and crossed his arms over his chest. "You should send a thank-you to your local drama teacher," he remarked, that gray gaze lingering on her face. "You're quite good."

"I don't know what you mean." Her lips betrayed her with a twitch and he didn't miss it.

"Aha! See, there we go. You're bullshitting me."

"Language," Rhiannon reminded him with a

significant nod over his shoulder. "Mrs. Parker will wallop you next time."

Still grinning, he leaned forward. "Give it up," he said. "I don't have time for this. Every minute I spend arguing with you is another minute I could be looking for Mr. Watson."

"You're having lunch," she said innocently. "I'm not wasting your time."

"But you will," he muttered ominously.

"Sorry?"

"I'll call you," he promised. "I will keep you apprised."

She shook her head. "That's not good enough. I have to help. I have to find him. He's like family to me." Her voice broke at the end and there was no drama intended. She didn't know what she would do without Theo. He was her rock, her very best friend.

Something in his expression shifted, softened, and Rhiannon took the opportunity to press her advantage.

"Have you been to Theo's house yet?" she asked.

"No." He grimaced. "Tad was supposed to leave me a key, but forgot. I can get in, of course, but I'd rather not have to break a window or screw up the lock."

She grinned. "I have a key."

"Have you been over there already?"

"Of course." She waited, forcing him to ask her what he wanted to know.

"Well?"

"Well what?"

He exhaled mightily. "Did you notice anything unusual? Check the messages on his machine? Was anything missing?"

No, she hadn't thought to check the messages on his machine and she wasn't altogether certain anything was missing, other than Theo. He had watered his plants, though, and stopped his mail. Martha, their carrier, had told her that. She should probably go back with him, Rhiannon realized. Much as it pained her to admit it, there were things he would likely think of that she wouldn't.

She thoughtfully chewed the inside of her cheek, then gave a brisk nod, deciding. "I did not check his messages," she said. She told him about the plants and the mail. "He would have taken copies of his grandfather's journals, I would imagine, though I didn't look to see if they were gone. We also need to check his luggage. See if he took the big case or a smaller one."

"We?" he drawled.

"We," she insisted. "Key, remember?"

"Fine." He relented. "I'll admit you'll be useful in this instance, so I will allow you to accompany me."

She rolled her eyes and picked up the check. Control freak. "Bet that high-handed attitude doesn't get you laid much," Rhiannon said, sliding out of the booth.

A startled chuckle broke up in his throat. "I don't need the attitude to get laid," he said, falling into step behind her.

She could feel his gaze on her ass and couldn't repress the smile sliding over her lips. "Yeah, you're right," she agreed with a lamentable sigh. "Probably best if you keep your mouth shut."

He guffawed. "I'll keep that in mind next time."

Rhiannon presented her check to the cashier. "Enjoyed it, Willie," she called back toward the kitchen.

Wilhelmina Malone lumbered into view, her dark face wreathed in her usual smile. "Glad to hear it, child. You get a piece of pie?"

"Better not," Rhiannon said, smacking her hip. "It'll end up right here." Or on her sizable ass, she thought.

While she never really dieted—she liked food too much for that—she nevertheless tried not to be a glutton. She could easily stand to lose ten to fifteen pounds, but the extra weight didn't bother her enough to motivate her to try. She actually liked being a little curvy. Women were supposed to be, dammit, despite what the current issue of *Vogue* said.

"Nonsense," Willie told her. "Help yourself and get a slice for your friend there, too." She looked Will up and down. "Looks like he could use a good piece of pie."

Between her telling him how to get a piece of ass and Willie telling him he needed a piece of pie, she was beginning to wonder if Will was starting to feel a bit abused.

"Thanks," she said, then shot Will a look over her shoulder as she made her way to the pie case. "Chocolate, lemon or pecan?" she asked.

"What are you having?"

"Chocolate."

"Then that's what I'll have."

Rhiannon peered into the case and *tsked* regretfully. "There's only one piece of chocolate left."

His lips twisted wryly. "Figures."

"You can have it," she told him. "I'd rather have the lemon." She put the slices of pie into a carton and snagged a couple of plastic forks from the cup on the counter.

He sighed. "I'll take the lemon. I'm not going to steal your pie."

He held open the front door for her and she

caught a whiff of some woodsy cologne. Nice, Rhiannon thought. The fragrance suited him.

"You can't steal it. It's a gift." She handed the carton to him.

He popped the lid and carved off a piece. "Being nice to me isn't going to do any good. You're still not coming with me."

Rhiannon took a bite of her own, savoring the meringue. "I wonder how many times you're going to have to say it before you start believing it?"

He stared at her mouth, seemingly distracted, then reached out and caught a piece of the fluffy dessert on her bottom lip against his thumb. Her gaze tangled with his and she carefully licked it off.

"You've got it backward," he said, his voice a bit strangled. "It's not how many times am I going to have to say it before *I* start believing it. It's how many times am I going to have to say it before *you* do."

Still rattled from the feel of his thumb against her tongue and how much she'd like to lick other parts of his body, Rhiannon grinned up at him. "In that case, you should save your breath."

He swore again.

5

THOUGH STILL OF ANTEBELLUM architecture, Theodore Watson's house was nothing like the grand Tara-like mansion his son called home. Built in the early 1820's, this was a simple white clapboard house. Four rooms downstairs, each boasting a single fireplace and divided by the customary wide hall, and three rooms upstairs.

Theo was a master gardener according to Rhiannon. The grounds were shaded with huge live oaks and magnolias, lots of creeping ivy and ornamental grasses. Rhododendrons and roses bloomed, adding a splash of color, and an entire area had been devoted to nothing but bird feeders, houses and baths.

The scent of dusty books, Old Spice and cherry pipe tobacco hung in the air and, while Will had never met Mr. Watson, something about the way

the older gentleman cared for his surroundings—
and the creatures that orbited through it—put him
in mind of his grandfather. John Forrester had been
well-read and had also had a soft spot for his feath-
ered friends.

Will wandered over to the fireplace and checked
out the pictures on the mantel. You could tell a lot
about a person by the images they chose to put on
display. A faded wedding photo was placed promi-
nently in the middle.

Rhiannon drifted to his side and nodded at the
picture. She stood so close that he could smell her.
Something light and orange. "That's Theo and
Sarah," she said, smiling. "He was a handsome
devil, wasn't he?"

Examining the happy couple, Will supposed he
was. He wasn't accustomed to making judgments
on manly looks. Nevertheless, the bride wore a
radiant smile and there was no denying the pride,
adoration and love in Theo's youthful expression.
Staring at the image—the pure emotion in their
eyes—made something strangely like envy curl
in his chest. *Ridiculous,* Will thought, batting the
feeling away like a pesky fly.

In truth, Will had always been so focused on his
career he'd never truly considered having a wife
and family—the whole dinner-at-five, church-on-
Sundays scenario. Had he ever been in love before?

Yes, once, in college and it had ended badly. She'd wanted a ring and he'd wanted to wait. He hadn't been ready to say I do, had been so engrossed in his career even then that he'd recognized on some level that it wouldn't have worked.

He'd balked and she'd bailed.

Since then he hadn't been with a woman who hadn't known going in that he was not interested in anything more than a little mutually satisfying recreational sex. He knew plenty of other soldiers who'd managed to make the marriage thing work, but had always known himself well enough to realize that, were he to have married, either the career or the marriage would have suffered, and that was unacceptable.

He'd chosen the career. *A smear of blood, a tiny hand...*

He swallowed hard and with difficulty, beat the images back. They were coming at him more frequently lately, Will realized with some dismay. He'd actually thought he was getting better at dealing with it, but...evidently not. He cleared his throat, aware that he'd been quiet entirely too long. He could feel Rhiannon's gaze on his face, examining him with those curiously perceptive eyes.

"And Sarah?" he asked. He expected he knew the answer to this question.

She inclined her head. "She died when Tad was eight. Aneurism." Her gaze lingered on the picture. "He never remarried. Said so long as his heart beat it would love her and it wouldn't be fair to another woman to only give her what was left." She smiled. "And believe me, lots of women tried. There's no telling how many book clubs were formed at the Begonia Public Library with the express purpose of putting its members in closer proximity to Theo."

That's right, Will thought. Watson had been the local librarian, as well, and he wondered how he'd found the time, particularly when he was also at the helm of the family business. Evidently he had good help in place—otherwise there was no way in hell the older man could get it all done. Especially with a miserable excuse of a son like Tad, who didn't appreciate the hard work, blood, sweat and tears that had gone into his heritage. Sheesh. Will liked that the plantation had stayed true to its roots and farmed almost all of the land. The fields were presently full of cotton, blanketing the earth in white.

Though it was his understanding that Tad was next in line to assume the CEO position, he could see where Watson wouldn't want to relinquish the reins to a greedy son who, apart from the house, had no interest in preserving his family's legacy and wasn't interested in helping worthy causes.

According to Rhiannon, Watson funded a local no-kill shelter, and offered numerous scholarships to aid local high school students who needed a little help to attend college. The parks and library had benefited from his benevolence, as well. Will grimaced. No doubt Tad would put an end to that if he ever got the opportunity.

His gaze skimmed along, looking at other pictures, then stopped short when he recognized a familiar face. Younger, of course, and sporting braces, but...

"That's you," he said, smiling. She'd been awkward, a bit shy looking, but the promise of beauty was there, even then.

"No cracks about the metal mouth," she warned him primly. "The end justified the means."

"You've known Theo a long time," he remarked. When she'd said he'd been a better father to her than her own, he'd just assumed she'd meant as an adult. He hadn't realized she'd known him since she was a child. Of course, that would explain the bond. He could tell that she genuinely loved the older gentleman.

"I have," she confirmed with a nod. "I was a bit of a freak growing up and spent a lot of time at the library. Theo and I shared a common quirk, which made me feel less like an outcast, and—" she sighed "—the rest is history."

She was being purposely vague, which naturally cued his curiosity. "A common quirk?"

"It's not important," she said, dismissing the question as though it wouldn't interest him. "The answering machine is in the kitchen. I'm going to check the messages, see if there's anything significant on there."

Now, that was odd, Will thought. The same woman who'd told him his attitude wouldn't get him laid often didn't want to share a "quirk"? Was she hiding some sort of physical flaw? A third breast? A sixth toe? His brooding gaze slid over her, making his pulse trip with desire. Wouldn't matter, Will decided. She'd still be the sexiest woman he'd ever laid eyes on.

Damn.

Had he had any idea that he was going to be presented with this sort of temptation, Will would have made a little time for sex before starting his new job. How long had it been? he wondered. Two, three months? Too damned long, obviously; otherwise he was certain he wouldn't be having this reaction to Rhiannon. He wouldn't be mentally stripping her naked and imagining her toned legs wrapped around his waist, her sexy mouth feeding at his. The mere scent of her wouldn't be driving him crazy and the riddle of her supposed quirk wouldn't spark his intense curiosity.

It was a pointless distraction, Will told himself, and futile, as well. He didn't have any business puzzling over her reticence to share her quirk, much less allowing himself to feel the desire currently sliding through his veins.

Theodore Watson had flown the coop, and it was his job to track him down.

The fact that he had to remind himself of this only irritated him further. Will ordinarily had the focus of a cobra and the tenacity of a bulldog.

It was her, he decided. She, with her hot-pink toes and delectable ass, was interfering with his ability to think.

Will abruptly decided that he needed to check in with the Triumvirate—damn Juan-Carlos for sticking that term in his brain—and see what proper protocol was for his present situation. He was supposed to make daily reports and, while he could simply forget to mention that Rhiannon Palmer was intent on following him to Philadelphia, it was a lie of omission he'd rather not have come back and bite him on the ass.

He unclipped the cell from his waist and hit number one on his speed-dial list. Juan-Carlos answered, of course, and he asked for Payne.

He seemed the least likely to rag his ass over his gorgeous, irritating little problem.

"How's it going, Will?" Payne asked by way of greeting.

"Slowly," he admitted. He brought him up to speed. "I'm at Theo's house now, poking around, but other than the fact that he's taken a small suitcase and copies of his great-great-grandfather's journals, I'm not having any luck. The family actually originated in Philadelphia and, considering the cash he took with him and the message he left Rhiannon Palmer, I'm assuming that he's headed there, or somewhere in between."

"You've met Ms. Palmer, then?" Not a trace of laughter betrayed his voice, but Will heard it all the same.

Will ducked into Theo's bedroom. "A little warning would have been nice, Payne," he hissed, annoyed that his new boss seemed to have purposely withheld some key information. Will liked having all the facts, dammit. How was he supposed to make good decisions without them? "I can't shake her," he admitted, swallowing the gall. "She's been following me all over town and is hell-bent on either tagging along with me or tailing me all the way to Philly."

Payne coughed to cover a poorly disguised

chuckle. "I was afraid she might become an issue."

"Issue, hell," he said. "She's a pain in the ass. How am I going to get rid of her? What's the protocol?"

"Are you sure you need to get rid of her? She knows your target and is familiar with this so-called treasure he's looking for."

Will leaned around the door frame to make sure she wasn't listening, then drew back. This was unexpected and he found himself strangely— stupidly—thrilled. "You think I ought to let her come with me?"

"I don't see what it could hurt. If she follows you, then she's just going to be a distraction. You take her with you and you can at least control the situation." He paused. "I've been in a similar position, Will." He laughed softly, seemingly remembering. "Take it from me, you're better off allowing her to come with you than her mucking along in your wake, screwing with your ability to focus."

Will barely repressed a snort. Either way she was going to screw with his focus. Even now, though she wasn't anywhere near him, he was still keenly aware of the fact that she was in the house, that she was close. He could *feel* her, as though her very heartbeat had the ability to ping him like sonar.

Theo and I share a common quirk.

That little mystery was going to drive him bat-shit crazy.

He swore, causing Payne to laugh.

"That bad, is she?"

"She's a beautiful nightmare," Will said honestly.

"And it would have been easier if she made a dog point?"

"Definitely." He couldn't impart enough dread into that one word.

"I see."

Good, then that made one of them.

"Regardless, my advice doesn't change. You're still better off taking her with you than allowing her to follow you. She could be useful."

Will exhaled mightily, stared at an Audubon print on the wall. "You're right, of course."

"Keep us posted."

"Will do," he said, then disconnected.

Damn. He was so screwed.

CHUCKLING UNDER HIS BREATH, Payne set the cordless phone back into the base and looked at the two expectant faces on the men whose attention had previously been on another Braves game.

"Let me guess," Flanagan said. "It's a woman."

"Rhiannon Palmer," Guy guessed correctly. "I knew she was going to be trouble."

"She's been tailing him," Payne told them. "Keeps insisting that she can help with the investigation."

"Can she?" Jamie asked.

"Possibly," Payne conceded. "I just think it's a little ironic, don't you?"

Guy lobbed a paper napkin ball at the trash can and gave a little *boo-yah* when it hit the mark. "What do you mean?"

"Seems there's an interfering woman involved in every case we've taken lately."

"True," Jamie admitted.

Guy released a tragic sigh. "And yet we keep marrying them."

SITTING IN THE PASSENGER SEAT of Will's Rubicon, Rhiannon inhaled the new-car scent and studied the atlas she had open on her lap. Since he'd finally come to his senses and gruffly announced that she could come with him—no idea what brought that on, but she didn't care because *she'd won*—she'd decided not to make taking her little hybrid a sticking point. She was just grateful to be doing something, to be contributing to the cause.

They'd stopped at a convenience store to stock a cooler—sodas and orange juice—and to snag a few snacks for the road. Will was a butterscotch Life Savers fan, and though there was absolutely no reason to find this little fact endearing, she did. She rolled her eyes and tried to pretend that she wasn't keenly aware of him, that she wasn't marveling over the strength in his hands or the competent way he handled the wheel. Both elicited a shiver.

Needing a distraction, Rhiannon pulled out her cell and dialed Theo's number again.

Will slid her a glance. "Who are you calling?"

"Theo," she said. Predictably, it connected to voice mail. She decided to leave another message. "Theo, you'd better call me the instant you get this. Please," she added. "I'm worried about you."

He quirked a brow. "Do you have caller ID?"

"Yes, why?"

"Did he leave the message on your machine from home or from his cell?"

"His cell, I think."

He merely nodded, snagged his own phone and placed a call. "What's his number?"

She rattled it off and he shared it with the people on the other end of the line. "Right," he said. "Let me know if you get any hits."

Ah, Rhiannon realized. He was tracking Theo's cell, trying to see which tower his last call was routed through. She nodded, impressed. "You're pretty good at this for someone who just started."

She watched his eyes crinkle at the corners with an almost smile. "Thank you."

"So were you in the security business before you started with the Ranger guys?"

"I guess you could say that," he replied, but didn't elaborate and, though he didn't so much as bat an eyelash, she felt a tenseness settle around him.

She chuckled, determined to draw him out. "That was a very vague answer."

He tapped his thumb against the steering wheel. "You'd know all about those."

She knew exactly what he was talking about, so didn't bother being coy. He'd been quite curious about her "shared-quirks" comment regarding her and Theo. While Rhiannon was a relatively vocal proponent of EI, she didn't exactly go around advertising her personal experiences with it.

Men, in particular, seemed unnerved by her special insight into their emotions, and intuition told her he'd be more spooked than the average guy. Probably because he wasn't just bringing along a little rolling case of baggage—he had a massive trunkful of it. Even now she could feel the weight of it pressing in on her, and she marveled at his ability to function at all.

Furthermore, she recognized this particular weight—it had all the hallmarks of death. The regret, the grief, the oppression. But who had he lost?

Rhiannon wondered. And better still, why did he blame himself?

"Truth uncomfortable for you?" he asked.

"Not at all," she said, shooting him a smile. "I let it drop, didn't I?"

"Surprisingly, yes. Only makes me more curious, though."

She grinned and pushed a lock of hair away from her face. "I know that feeling, as well."

"I was in the military," he said. "Army. A Ranger."

So she'd been right. He was military. And a Ranger? Those guys were usually in service for life. Too much time spent training to simply change their mind. Something must have happened, Rhiannon decided, studying him from the corner of her eye.

And that something was directly related to his pain.

"The hair was sort of a tip-off," she said. "Well, that and the fact that you're bossy."

He chuckled. "I'm used to giving orders."

"*I'm* not one of your soldiers."

His gaze lingered over her legs, drifted along her hip, slid over her breasts and ultimately settled on her mouth. A bark of ironic laughter rumbled from his throat. "Believe me, I am well aware of that."

Holy hell, Rhiannon thought as the tops of her thighs caught fire. Her nipples tingled and she felt short of breath, as if the heat between them was sucking all the oxygen out of the car. She'd been feeling that off him, too—the desire—but clearly he'd been trying to control it, as well. And when that control slipped...

Damn.

"S-so you're happy with the career change?"

"I will be so long as you don't get me fired," he muttered.

"I will not get you fired," she promised him. "I'm here to help you."

He merged onto the interstate, headed north and heaved a fatalistic sigh. "So you've said."

"Haven't I been helpful so far? Didn't I let you in Theo's house and tell you everything that I know?"

"You have."

She settled more firmly against the seat. "You'll see," she said primly. "We're going to make an excellent team."

"Rah, rah," he cheered with bored enthusiasm. *Smart-ass,* she thought, reluctantly impressed with his humor. Probably because it was similar to her own.

"We should probably go through Chattanooga," Rhiannon told him. "Theo's great-grandmother was from Soddy-Daisy."

"Soddy-Daisy? You just made that up, didn't you?"

"Of course not." She showed him the map. "It's right here. See?"

A pained expression settled over his gorgeous face. "Why do I get the feeling we're going to have to dismember every limb on Theo's family tree in order to find him?"

"Probably because we are."

He harrumphed. "What's the significance of the Bible verse?"

"Ah," she said. "Mortimer Watson was a very devout man and his diaries are littered with his spiritual reflections and various Bible verses. The significance of Matthew 6:21 is that its only appearance is two weeks before the Union troops marched through Begonia on their way to Atlanta."

Will inclined his head. "I see."

"Theo has known that the verse was a significant clue and we've scoured records and diaries trying to find any reference to the word *heart*."

"And you didn't find anything?"

"No…but evidently Theo has."

A thought struck. "And wherever he's gone, he's taken his metal detector with him. It usually sits by the back door, and it wasn't there when I went to check the messages on his machine."

"So he's digging, then?"

"That's my guess. Lord knows he's practically taken the house apart and dug from one end of the Watson Plantation to the other." She chuckled. "Tad nearly had a fit when Theo tore up the hearth."

Will's incredulous gaze found hers. "You're kidding me, right?"

"I wish." She closed the atlas and tucked it into the side pocket of her door. "It was a relatively common hiding place, you know? People would bury their valuables beneath the hearth, mortar back over it and then their goods were safe in the event of fire." She smiled, remembering. "Theo had thought *heart* and *hearth* were close enough in spelling, so he took apart every fireplace on the lower floors."

"He's determined, isn't he?"

"He's always been convinced it was real. He's been actively searching for more than sixty years."

"That's dedication."

She smiled fondly, picturing her friend's lined, dear face. "That's Theo."

"Wonder why he didn't tell you where he was going?"

She'd wondered that, as well, and could only assume that he'd left in such a hurry he hadn't wanted to wait until she'd finished her class for the day. As she'd just said, he'd been looking for this for sixty years. Waiting another moment would have been impossible for him.

She shared as much. "I don't think there was any real purpose behind not telling me. I think he just got excited and went directly into treasure-hunter mode." She gazed out the window, stared at the passing scenery. "And if it weren't for the diabetes, I wouldn't be concerned at all. I know that he's avoiding Tad and I'm a mere casualty of that. But I just can't shake the feeling that something terrible could happen to him and no one would be there to help him, you know?"

Will was silent for a moment. "We'll find him," he said reassuringly.

We, she thought, glad that he was finally coming around. Her heart warmed.

"Thanks. I needed to hear that."

"So where do we start?" Will asked. "What are we looking for in Soddy-Daisy?"

"Relatives, old family home places and graves," she said.

"That covers a lot of ground," Will remarked, staring straight ahead.

"But it makes sense, given the cash he took with him. He's looking for family treasure. It only makes sense that he'd go where his people were from." Or at least it did to her.

He nodded and shot her a resigned smile. "So how much farther to Soddy-Daisy?"

6

THIS WAS PRECISELY WHY he didn't want her tagging along with him, Will thought as he finally settled into his rented bed for the night. Rhiannon was in the room next to him, and though he knew she was probably still fully clothed and not doing anything particularly sexy, he nevertheless knew she was there.

So he pictured her naked.

As if on cue, her shower started.

Bloody hell.

Sleek, wet skin, back arched into the spray, rivulets of water cascading over the heavy globes of her breasts, clinging to rosy nipples. Dark hair tangled down her back, darker hair between her thighs…

He shifted as he went uncomfortably hard, then determinedly began to translate the TV Guide into

Spanish to try to occupy his mind. When Spanish didn't work, he moved to Russian. He'd just finished the eleven-o'clock listings when her shower finally—blessedly—went off.

But she was still naked, still wet, and he knew it.

His dick jerked hard against his zipper and he speared his hands through his hair and gave a sharp tug.

It was at that precise moment that he heard a tentative knock on their adjoining door.

Shit.

He scrambled up and tried to think of a convincing way to cover up his hard-on—his dick was practically peeping out the top of his jeans. Then, in a moment of inspiration, he quickly untucked his shirt and hoped that it wouldn't betray him.

He opened the door, and the scent of warm oranges abruptly washed over him. "Yes?" he asked in a voice that wasn't altogether steady.

She was partially hidden behind the door, her hand securing the towel behind her back. Unfortunately—or fortuitously, however one decided to look at it—her bare, heart-shaped rear end was reflected in the room's slightly foggy mirror, giving him an unobstructed view of the most beautiful ass he'd ever seen. He instantly imagined his hands on her rump as he pushed into her from behind, the smooth indentation of her spine.

"I forgot to pack toothpaste," she said, wincing. "Do you mind if I borrow yours?"

Water clung to her eyelashes and her nose was shiny. It was small, he realized now. Quite possibly the most petite nose he'd ever seen. How had he missed that? And why in God's name did he find that so endearing?

"Er...sure," he said, trying to untangle his thoughts. He darted to his bathroom and pulled a travel tube from his case. "Here you go," he said, handing it over.

"Thanks," she said. "I'd wait a few minutes before I showered if I were you. The hot water's a little iffy."

He nodded. "Noted."

"I'll give this right back, if you want to leave the door open."

For reasons he didn't understand, she seemed reluctant to leave. "Sure," he said, for lack of anything better.

She grinned again, then partially closed her door. Seconds later he heard the telltale sounds of the rest of her evening routine.

Will blew out the breath he hadn't realized he'd been holding and sagged against the wall, the memory of her ass still clinging determinedly in his mind. He massaged his temples, valiantly holding on to what remained of his sanity.

Damn. This was *so* not good.

He could *not* act on this attraction. It would be the pinnacle of stupidity, the absolute height of idiocy. New job, first assignment. He couldn't afford to fuck it up.

Too important. No place else to go. He'd be rudderless, without a purpose. The thought terrified him.

While not strictly a part of this investigation, she was a crucial key to whether or not he was able to see it through.

Distance, Will told himself. He had to be with her when they were in the car—he was trapped. But his evenings had to be his own. And the next time they booked a hotel room, he'd make sure they were on a different damned floors, not in adjoining rooms. He couldn't keep torturing himself by listening to her bathe, wishing he could join her. Imagining filling his hands with her breasts, filling the rest of her with himself.

"Here ya go," she said, handing the tube of toothpaste back. "Hey, I'm not exactly tired. Wanna watch a movie on pay-per-view later? After you have your shower maybe?"

"Sure," he said, wondering if he could cut his tongue out with a blunt object. Hadn't he just resolved to stay away from her? Hadn't he just determined that she was too much temptation? That he'd go through hell trying to resist her if he didn't stay away from her?

Yes, he had.

And it hadn't made one whit of difference.

She smiled at him, her unusual eyes lighting up. "Great. I'll pop over later, then."

Rather than lie on the bed and brood about his own stupidity, Will labeled the small thrill of anticipation dread and climbed into the shower. It was a movie, he told himself. Harmless enough, right? They'd watch the film—he'd purposely choose something he knew she'd hate, like *Blood 'N Guts IV*—then he could send her on her way. She'd go back to her bed. He would stay in his. He would keep his hands to himself and everything would be fine.

Ten minutes later Rhiannon came strolling into his room with two of the pillows from her bed, a couple of soft drinks she'd snagged from the vending machine, two bags of chips and two packets of M&M's. She quickly made her nest on his side of the bed, then handed him his portion of the snacks.

"I'd rather have popcorn and chocolate, but the chips will do in a pinch," she said, as though they did this all the time. She sighed happily and tossed him the remote. "What's that cologne you're wearing?" she asked, sniffing the air appreciatively.

"Bulgari," he said, startled by the abrupt subject change.

"It's woodsy," she said. "With a hint of pepper. Nice."

He hadn't given it much thought beyond the fact that he liked it. "Thanks." He settled in next to her, careful to keep a pillow between them. She wore a pair of striped boxer shorts and a little tank top. No bra.

His mouth watered.

She'd pulled her hair up into a giant knot on her head and looked completely relaxed and at ease. Clearly she was not as uncomfortably aware of him as he was of her, Will thought, annoyed once again.

Was she attracted to him? Yes, gratifyingly, he knew she was. He'd seen her eyes darken with interest, had watched her gaze linger over his mouth. She was equally intrigued…but obviously had better control.

It infuriated him.

He was *always* the one in control.

Because he was incapable of thinking rationally, he removed the pillow and slid an inch or so in her direction, purposely tilting the mattress until she leaned toward him, as well.

Her breath gave a little hitch and he smiled, marginally mollified.

"So," he said, aiming the remote at the television, "what do you want to watch?"

"Doesn't matter," she said. "I'm not picky."

He selected *Saw III* and waited for her reaction.

Because she was the most unpredictable creature he'd ever met, her eyes lit up. "Ooh, a horror movie. Blood and guts. My favorite." She popped a chip into her mouth.

He laughed and shook his head. "You are one odd girl, you know that?"

"I'm unique," she corrected. "*Odd* makes me sound like a freak. *Unique* means I'm charming."

"Can't you be a charming freak?"

She shushed him. "The movie's starting."

He laughed, surprised. "It's the previews."

"I know. I like them."

"We're not going to talk at all?"

She heaved a put-upon sigh. "No, because we're watching a movie," she said with exaggerated patience, as though she were explaining this to a half-wit.

"Then why didn't you just watch it alone? What's the point of watching it together?"

She looked over at him and smiled. "So that we

can share the experience, then talk about it when it's over. That work for you?"

He chewed the inside of his cheek to keep from smiling. "Yes, it will."

She nodded. "Good."

Only it didn't work, because thirty minutes into the movie she was sound asleep, curled up on her side, her delightfully distracting rump pressing into his hip.

Will groaned.

Her breath came in even little puffs and a single strand of hair had fallen down and curled over her smooth cheek. He was suddenly hit with the almost overwhelming urge to tuck it behind her ear, but was afraid that if he touched her, he wouldn't be able to stop. She was quite honestly the most compelling person he'd ever been around in his life. Sexy and open, outrageous, charming and, yes, odd.

Rhiannon Palmer was different.

He couldn't exactly put his finger on what made her so special, but he knew it all the same.

She was an unknown quantity. Dangerous.

And if he didn't keep his distance, he was doomed.

With a reluctant sigh, Will carefully rolled away from her, snagged one of the pillows and let himself into her room. The scent of oranges still hung in the air and her lacy bra dangled from the doorknob. He shook his head, settled into her bed and then looked heavenward.

"I'd better get points for this," he muttered. "Because this is *not* funny."

SORRY ABOUT RUNNING YOU out of your bed last night," Rhiannon said as she sprinkled golden raisins over her oatmeal the next morning. "I must have been more tired than I realized."

She had to have been; otherwise she would never have fallen asleep like that, particularly when she'd been so miserably aware of him. Honestly, she'd taken one whiff of that cologne, aftershave or shower gel—who knew which one?—and had become strangely intoxicated with the scent. It had made her want to slowly stalk him to the bed, then lick him all over. Between the scent and his own personal magnetism she'd been a basket case within seconds of walking into the room.

Then he'd gone and moved that pillow, forcing her slightly against him, and her arm had practically caught fire. He was quite frankly the sexiest man she'd ever been around in her life, and the need hammering through her blood with every beat of her heart was simply relentless.

She wanted him.

With an intensity that walked the fine edge of dangerous and debilitating.

Ordinarily when Rhiannon wanted something—or in this case some*one*—she didn't hesitate. Life was too short for regrets, and happiness too often was fleeting. While she wouldn't call herself a total hedonist, she nevertheless wasn't accustomed to denying herself.

But for whatever reason—self-preservation, maybe?—she was hesitant to act on this particular attraction.

There was an edge here, an intensity she wasn't altogether certain of, and that peculiar sensation coupled with her unusual instantaneous fondness for him made her slightly…leery. Factor in the haunting sadness emanating from him and she was certain she could become entirely too involved, or at the very least, involved on an unfamiliar level she had no desire to tread.

She could easily see herself getting…attached to him.

In the first place, she didn't want to be attached. Too much emotional insecurity in investing personal happiness in another person for her comfort. And in the second place, were she to develop any sort of lingering interest in him, she instinctively knew she'd scare him to death. Like her, she sensed he wasn't looking for anything permanent.

Which should have made him perfect. And yet she hesitated.…

Having consumed enough eggs to send his cholesterol into the danger zone, Will merely leaned back and shook his head. "No problem," he said. "Same bed, different room."

"Any updates this morning?" she asked. "Any news on that cell tower?"

He nodded. "He was still in town."

"Damn."

"Any other hits?"

"None," he said. "Which means he's probably turned it off."

She grimaced. "Or let the battery go dead. He's horrible about that. But at least we know we're on the right track," she reminded him.

The freshly cut flowers they'd found on Theo's relatives' graves yesterday had his signature thoughtfulness written all over them. The ground was unbroken, indicating that he hadn't found what he was looking for there, but she had no doubt that it was he who had placed the relatively new blooms on those plots.

And then there'd been the penny, of course.

She smiled, remembering. Because he shared his thoughts with people whether they asked for them or not, Theo always had a pocketful of pennies to give to those with whom he shared his opinions. Sarah's headstone, in particular, was always covered in pennies.

"So what do you think our next move should be?" Will asked her.

She blinked with exaggerated wonder. "You're asking me?"

"I wouldn't have had any idea to look for Theo in Soddy-Daisy, much less that the flowers and coins left on those graves were his doing." He took a sip of water. "So, yes, I am asking you."

Self-satisfied pleasure expanded in her chest. "Because you need me?" she pressed. "Because I am helpful? Just like I said I would be."

"You're a helpful distraction," he conceded, his cheek lifting in a too-charming half smile. She couldn't get over his eyes, Rhiannon thought, once again struck by their unique shade. A bright silvery-gray.

She chuckled and leaned forward. "How exactly am I distracting you? By offering my assistance? By being your navigator? By telling you that you're eating too many eggs and not enough fiber?" She determinedly scooped up another bite of oatmeal, setting a good example for his benefit.

She knew exactly how she was distracting him, of course. She was equally distracted, and for the same damned reason.

Lust.

He frowned at her plate. "Oatmeal is nasty. I'd rather eat a cardboard box."

"We should pick up some fiber bars when we stop for my toothpaste."

"I don't mind sharing," he said. There was an undercurrent to his voice she didn't fully understand.

She shook her head. "I prefer my own brand."

He snorted and rolled his eyes. "Why am I not surprised?"

"There's nothing wrong with yours," she said. "Most people like their breath minty fresh."

He slid her a sardonic look. "And you don't?"

"Mint makes me gag. I prefer oranges and cloves."

"Mint makes you gag?" he asked, slightly incredulous. His lips twisted. "Bet that made for some interesting kissing sessions, huh?"

Her gaze involuntarily dropped to his lips and she felt her own mouth tingle in response. She'd bet he was one hell of a kisser. "Only when a guy dosed up on something strong. Usually the taste is too faint to trigger the reflex."

"Little favors, eh? That could definitely give a guy a complex. Finally build up the courage to make his move and you gag on him."

She chuckled at his analogy. "It's not like I can help it, you know," she said. "It's just…too strong."

"It's supposed to be," he told her. "How else is one supposed to fight bad breath?"

She narrowed her gaze in playful censure. "Are you saying my breath is bad because I don't use minty toothpaste?"

He fought a grin and his gaze drifted over her lips. "I won't know until you've tried it, will I?"

"Fine," she said drolly. "Tonight after I brush my teeth, I'll be sure to breathe on you."

This line of conversation could *so* get her into trouble. It felt too much like flirting and not enough like harmless banter.

Naturally she found it thrilling.

The grin that tugged at his lips? *Pure sin.* "I'll look forward to it."

Perversely, so did she.

7

"THEO WAS HERE a couple of days ago," Mimi Watson said. "I was surprised, of course. Haven't seen him in years."

"Was he just visiting, Miss Mimi, or was there a specific reason he came by?" Rhiannon asked the elderly woman.

Mimi's faded blue eyes were warm as she worked the crochet needles between her arthritic fingers. "Oh, he just wanted to chat. Said he was working on a genealogy chart, a new hobby of his, and wanted to pick my brain about some of our relatives."

Rhiannon sent him a significant look. "Really? Which ones was he interested in?"

She corrected a bad stitch. "All of them, really, but he was particularly interested in where Mrs. Amelia Watson was buried. Oh, and little Winston, of course." She *tsked* under her breath. "The infant mortality rate was terrible in those days," she said sadly. "Moving south was not an easy journey for old Uncle Mortimer. Buried a wife and child on the way. The child first, of course. The pox. Amelia grieved herself to death. She's buried in Kingsport, I believe. Wasn't sure about Winston, but like I told Theo, I think they lost him somewhere around Roanoke."

"That's terrible," Rhiannon commiserated softly, and Will could tell the news affected her on a deeper than ordinary level. Almost as if it was her own family.

A puzzled frown wrinkled her forehead. "Theo has shared a lot of your family history with me over the years. So Mortimer must have been married before then? Sophia was his second wife?"

"That's right. He missed his family terribly, you see. The story I've always heard was Miss Sophia was a very jealous woman and destroyed all the pictures of Mortimer's late wife. Guess she knew that Amelia would always have his heart, that she was the substitute wife."

Always have his heart, Will thought. That certainly sounded like a significant clue.

And once again he had to hand it to Rhiannon. She'd spent several minutes going over the atlas this morning, searching for places along their route to Philadelphia that Theo had mentioned. She'd hit pay dirt with Sweetwater, pulled out her BlackBerry and used the mobile phone book to pull up all the Watsons. She'd found Mimi and instantly recognized the name as one Theo had mentioned.

Mimi Watson had at least a decade on her nephew, but lived alone in a small cottage downtown. She wore a trendy sportswear outfit in shades of lavender and her snowy-white hair was set into a sweeping, puffy style. Her lined cheeks were powdered to perfection and bright pink lipstick painted her mouth. Her white tennis shoes didn't show the faintest scuff and gleamed against the green indoor-outdoor carpeting covering her front porch. She epitomized a genteel Southern lady and, though they didn't have the time, he could have listened to her tell stories in her lovely drawl all day long.

Rhiannon laid her hand on Mimi's knee. "Mimi, thank you so much for all your help. It's a relief to know that Theo was here and was fine."

"Silly boy," she said, disapproval coloring her tone. "He should have let you know where he was going. People tend to worry when their old folks just vanish. Poor Tad must be a wreck with nerves," she fretted.

Rhiannon delicately avoided answering by asking instead, "He was here day before yesterday, you say?"

"Yes. I insisted that he stay for dinner, of course, and you know Theo." She gestured to a vase of flowers. "He's always so thoughtful."

Rhiannon grinned. "Yes, he is." She nodded once. "Well, Miss Mimi, we'd better be on our way."

"Good luck finding him, dear. I'm sure he's fine. You let me know when you run him to ground, you hear?"

"Absolutely."

Rhiannon gave her a quick hug and, feeling strangely out of place, Will merely nodded once.

"Okay," she said with a heavy breath when they were once again in the car. "We've got our next destination."

He backed out of the drive. "Kingsport."

"Yes." She pushed her hands through her hair. "But I don't think we're going to find him there."

Will didn't, either. They were only about three hours from Kingsport and Theo had left almost two days ago. If he'd found what he was looking for in that town, then they would have heard from him by now. Clearly he hadn't, and he had moved on.

"So you'd never heard of the first wife? Amelia?"

She shook her head. "Not that I can recall."

"Do you think Theo knew of her?"

"I don't think so," she said, her tone thoughtful. "He must have found something. He's been going through some old boxes, had found them tucked away in the corner of the attic in the cottage there on the plantation. It was the first house, you see. The temporary home while the plantation home was being built."

Will considered that. "Then why doesn't Theo live there? Why move to town?"

She leaned her head against the back of the seat and rolled her neck toward him. A smile played over her ripe mouth. "The official reason? Because his estate manager needs to live on site. The real reason? He's convinced it's haunted."

Will chuckled. "Haunted? But wouldn't he be related to this particular ghost?"

"Doesn't matter," Rhiannon said. "He still gets spooked."

"Who is it?"

"Interestingly enough…it's Sophia."

A bark of laughter rumbled from his throat. "But she sounds like such a sweet, understanding lady."

Rhiannon scowled. "She sounds like a bitter old bitch to me, but what do I know?"

His lips twitched. "Don't hold back. Tell me what you really think."

"Do I strike you as the kind of person who holds back?"

Will shook his head. "You absolutely do not," he admitted. "You're frighteningly...honest. It's refreshing, actually." And he meant it. No doubt a person never had to wonder where they stood with her. Furthermore, though he'd laughed at the fact that she was a guidance counselor, he could easily see how kids would readily warm to her. She was frank without being cruel and there was a comforting quality, despite her obvious energy, that literally compelled a person to want to be close to her. To confide in her.

Mimi was a perfect example. Rhiannon had never met the woman before in her life and yet within three minutes of being in her company, Mimi had acted as if they were old friends. Rhiannon had been able to garner the older woman's trust with enviable ease. Had he been asking the same questions—alone—Will didn't think he would have fared so well. Just another reminder of how much she was genuinely helping him.

Distracting him, too, of course. He could never forget that. Take now, for instance. Her warm citrusy scent—it must be in her shampoo, too, Will thought—swirled around his senses and the yellow-

and-white checked top she wore showcased her pear-shaped breasts to absolute perfection. She wore a denim skirt that was long enough to be appropriate but short enough to make him sweat, and a silver chain loaded with star charms dangled around her ankle.

Because he was a nosy bastard, he'd taken a cursory look at her toiletries in her bathroom this morning and realized that she hadn't brought a single bit of makeup, only a small tube of tinted organic lip balm. Hell, she'd gone to sleep with her hair in a damp ball on her head and woken up this morning looking as though she could have shot a shampoo commercial. She was effortlessly sexy, and something about that made her all the more appealing.

And minty toothpaste made her gag. He laughed under his breath, remembering.

She shot him a look. "Something funny?"

Just you, he thought.

And clearly he was an idiot...because while she'd been stocking up on fiber bars and bagged popcorn—she'd had a craving—at the drugstore this morning, he'd snuck to the photo-center cash register and purchased a new tube of toothpaste.

One that wouldn't make her gag.

And a box of condoms.

FINDING AMELIA WATSON took a bit more effort, but after a vital-records search using various spellings of Amelia's name, they finally got a hit.

Rhiannon stood at the foot of the grave and felt a pang of regret for the woman who had grieved herself to death over the loss of her child. Theo's flowers—only slightly wilted this time—were nestled against the chalky, weathered headstone.

"Another penny?" Will asked. "Is this the quirk you were talking about? Do you and Theo leave pennies on headstones?"

Half of her mouth hitched up in a grin. "Nice try, but no."

"Damn."

"Theo likes to share his thoughts, whether he's asked for them or not," she explained. "He's just being courteous."

He arched a skeptical brow. "You mean he talked to Amelia's marker?"

She studied the headstone. *Beloved wife and mother.* "In a manner of speaking."

"No wonder you're so close to him. You're both—"

She shot him a glare, silently urging him to rethink what he was about to say.

"Unique," he finished, smiling.

She nodded primly. "You're learning."

"We're closing the gap," he said. "Getting closer."

Which was true, yet she could still feel an unexplained sense of urgency. Rhiannon was by no means psychic—clairvoyance was not her talent—but she knew well enough to trust her instincts, and those same instincts now were telling her that she needed to find Theo before something terrible happened. An unexplained ball of dread sat in her belly, a constant reminder that they needed to push on.

"So he obviously didn't dig here," Will said, inspecting the undisturbed grass.

"No need if the metal detector didn't give him any indication there was a reason to."

"True," he conceded. He inspected the sky, in particular the low orange ball of sun sinking to the western horizon. "We're less than three hours from Roanoke. We should probably get on the road."

He was right, she knew. They would need to get an early start tomorrow. She'd also done an online search for Winston Watson's marker—or records of any sort—and hadn't found the first thing. Of course, she'd done only a cursory search. It didn't mean nothing was there—it just meant she hadn't had time to look properly.

Unfortunately, if finding Winston's marker was easy, then she suspected she would have heard from

Theo already. He'd had at least a thirty-six-hour jump on them and obviously was still searching. Poor record keeping, lost or destroyed documents... there were so many things that could have gone wrong over the years.

Rhiannon let go a small breath. "This is going to be like looking for a needle in a haystack."

"Yeah." He passed a hand over his face. "And Mimi said 'around Roanoke.' That leaves a lot of ground."

Yes, it did. And Rhiannon wasn't entirely sure where they should start.

Will stooped, picked a dandelion from the ground and twirled it between his fingers. "Theo was a librarian, right? He knows those systems better than any of the other more advanced technologies out there now, I would assume?"

She considered him. "Yes."

"Then he's probably relying on old obits from newspapers stored on microfiche."

She brightened. "You're right. He's competent on the computer, but he is much more at home in the library."

"So we start with the libraries on the fringes of Roanoke and tighten our circle. Work from the outside in."

She smiled at him, impressed. "That's an excellent plan."

His lips lifted with droll humor. "I do have them on occasion." He laid the bloom on the headstone. "Are you hungry?"

She gave him a duh look. "Do you even have to ask?"

His chuckle was low and sexy. "We need to find a sandwich bar with Wi-Fi," he said. "Get a list of libraries and start mapping our route."

Rhiannon headed for his Jeep. "You're on a roll."

"Smart-ass."

Twenty minutes later Will had his laptop open and had begun the search. He'd ordered an enormous sandwich and waffle fries and was periodically taking bites between searches.

He grimaced. "There are a lot of little libraries around here," he said, scrutinizing the screen.

Rhiannon popped a bite of artichoke into her mouth. "How many?"

"More than twenty on the fringes, and that's not including the city."

"No wonder we haven't heard from Theo."

"Yes, but I think we can gain some ground. I imagine he's just wandering from town to town making inquiries and checking cemeteries along the way. We have a plan."

"Are we going to check the cemeteries, as well?"

He shrugged. "It couldn't hurt. There are a lot of deaths that never make it into the obituaries. Particularly if they weren't local and were simply passing through, you know?"

Rhiannon's eyes widened significantly as she digested that. "We're going to be spending a lot of time in your car."

His eyes twinkled and he cocked his head. "Mine might not be as economically friendly as yours, but it's got more legroom."

She couldn't argue there. And he was an excellent driver. He expertly negotiated traffic and, though it was ridiculous, she'd found her gaze riveted on the way his hands rested against the steering wheel—the large palms and long, blunt-tipped fingers, the masculine muscles and veins that made his arms so very different from hers. A breath stuttered out of her lungs as she imagined them wrapped around her, his skillful hands on her body.

"It's nice," she said, trying to distract herself from that line of thinking. "And really new. When did you get it?"

"A couple of days ago."

"So you would have wanted to drive regardless."

He made another notation on the map and added

an address. "I would have wanted to drive even if I'd been in a tank."

She grinned. "He who has the keys has the power, eh?"

"Something like that," he admitted, still focused on his task.

"So how much longer are we driving before we settle in for the night?"

"I thought we could put in another hour on the road. You up for that?"

"Sure." Though she was a bit worn out. The endless time in the car, the stress of worrying over Theo and the unceasing attraction—being constantly aware of and in tune with every move he made, every breath that entered and exited his lungs—was beginning to get to her. She needed a little distance. A chance to regroup. To possibly desensitize herself.

As if that would help, she thought fatalistically.

She was hopelessly in lust with him, had been fantasizing about him all day. In bed, against a wall, in the shower. Didn't matter. She just wanted, and there was nothing tender or gentle about the sentiment. She wanted the hot, desperate, mindless sort of sex that resulted in frantic disrobing, torn underwear and whisker burn. Her skin prickled with heat and she squirmed in her seat as her sex tingled with warmth.

"Are you okay?" he asked, looking up at her.

"Sure. Why?"

"You look a little flushed."

Busted. "My sandwich is hot."

He smiled, the wretch, as though he knew she was lying. "Want me to blow on it?"

"With your minty breath? No, thank you."

He laughed and his gaze drifted slowly over her mouth. "Still going to breathe on me?"

"Yes," she said, her toes curling at the thought. "If for no other reason than to prove to you that mint isn't the only option when it comes to fighting bad breath. We've been brainwashed with advertising to believe otherwise, I know, but—" she sighed as though it were a tragic injustice "—it simply isn't true."

His lips twitched. "I'm surprised you haven't mounted some sort of campaign," he said. "Launched a Web site or blogged about it."

She tossed her napkin onto her plate and grabbed her purse from the back of the chair. "How do you know I haven't? Now, if you'll excuse me, I'm going to brush my teeth."

8

THREE CHAIN HOTELS LATER, they finally found one that passed muster. Hotel number one had a surly desk clerk who displayed poor personal hygiene and hotel number two had, according to his companion, "smelled funny."

It would not do.

This one, however, boasted the clean scent of lemon cleaning solution and had a huge vase of purple irises—her favorites, she'd explained—on the check-in counter, and she was certain it would do nicely.

Will watched her lean over and sniff the blooms, and the small smile that captured her lips made his own inexplicably slide into a halfhearted grin. For someone with such high standards, the littlest things made her happy. She was a conundrum, Will thought, with more facets to her personality than the most complexly cut diamond.

"I love this shade," she said, fingering a bloom as the desk clerk located their rooms. "It's the color of my bedroom."

"Purple?"

"More lilac I would say," she told him, as if he would understand the difference. She lifted her foot and absently rubbed the back of her calf. Her long curly hair was once again pushed away from her face and secured with her ridiculously large sunglasses. They swallowed her face and looked especially bizarre with that tiny little nose.

Naturally, because he was quickly losing any perspective—provided he'd ever had it to start with—he found it charming.

"You're in luck," the desk clerk said. "We've got one room left."

Rhiannon blinked and her mouth rounded in a little O of surprise. She looked at him, then back to the clerk. "Only one?"

"Oh, you're not together?" the clerk asked.

"We're traveling together," Will explained before this could get any more awkward.

She smiled regretfully. "I'm afraid it's all I've got. It's a double," she said. "If that makes any difference."

To his amazement, Rhiannon merely shrugged.

"I'm cool with that, if you are," she said, as though sharing a room with him wasn't the least bit disconcerting. "It's late and I'm tired."

"I'm fine with it," he said. He slid a credit card to the desk clerk. "I just didn't expect you to be."

She blinked up at him, her eyes innocently surprised. "Why not? I'm much more logical than you."

An incredulous laugh broke apart in his throat. "You are *so* full of shit."

She *tsked* under her breath. "Cursing again. You've got a terrible mouth."

He grinned at her. "But it's minty fresh."

"You're on the second floor," the clerk told him, handing him the key card. Her lips twitched. "Elevators are just around that corner. Continental breakfast is served from six to ten. Enjoy your stay."

He nodded his thanks, then slung his bag over his shoulder and reached for Rhiannon's.

"I've got it." She grabbed it and they headed toward the elevators. "Honestly, it's on wheels."

He depressed the call button. "I was trying to be nice."

"I know." She sighed as though it were a bad thing. "You open doors and pull out chairs and everything. A girl could get used to that kind of old-fashioned courtesy."

They stepped into the elevator and his gaze slid to her once more. So the guys she typically dated weren't always as polite? Interesting...

"Courtesy doesn't ever go out of fashion," he said. An image of his grandfather sprang to mind and he smiled. "At least, not according to my grandfather."

The doors slid open and he waited for her to pass. She looked at him over her shoulder. "Sounds like he's a smart man."

"He was," Will confirmed. He scanned the hall for their room number.

Her gaze softened and a sympathetic frown lined her brow. "I'm sorry."

"Cancer." He sighed, slipping the key card into the slot. "Damned miserable disease. We lost him five years ago." He was glad he'd made the time to call his grandmother today. She'd been thrilled to hear from him, her familiar voice damning him when it broke on the verge of tears. Though she was smart enough to know that something terrible had sent him fleeing from the military, she didn't know what, and Will was determined never to tell her. It was hard enough living with it himself. He'd be damned before he off-loaded it on her.

"Both of my grandparents died when I was very young, so I never knew them," she said. "I was always envious of people who did."

Will flipped on a light. "Mine raised me," he told her, for reasons he couldn't begin to explain. This wasn't something he ordinarily talked about. Not because it was painful or he had anything to hide—he just never felt the need to share. It was her, he realized again. She just had that way about her.

She rolled her bag up against the wall, dropped her purse on the low dresser and turned to face him. "Really?"

She didn't ask why, just left him the choice as to whether or not he wanted to tell her. He liked that. "Yeah," he said, rubbing the back of his neck. "My parents and little brother were killed in a car accident when I was ten."

She gasped. "Will, that's horrible. I'm so sorry."

"It was a long time ago."

"Were you in the accident, as well?"

"No. I was at school. David, my little brother, had a doctor's appointment that day. Asthma," he explained. "A truck ran a light and hit them."

Her face crumpled. "Damn."

Because he couldn't stand the sadness on her face, he purposely laughed to lighten the moment. "Who has the potty mouth now?"

It worked. She smiled. "Yes, but at least it's not polluted with mint." She gave a delicate shiver.

He shook his head and gestured toward the beds. "Which one do you want?"

"The one farthest from the door, if you don't mind. You can have the death bed."

His eyes rounded and he knew he was going to regret asking, but couldn't help himself all the same. "The death bed?"

She plopped down on her bed and leaned back, testing the mattress. "Yes," she said. "If we're attacked in the middle of the night, more than likely the intruder will come after you first because you're closest to the door." She sat up again and her hair settled around her shoulders. "And that will give me the opportunity to escape."

Will felt the edges of his mouth tremble. "You've given this a lot of thought, haven't you?"

She kicked off her shoes and happily flexed her toes. "No more than anything else."

"And you wouldn't try to save me? You'd just run?"

She considered him for a moment, then released a small sigh. "I would probably try to save you," she admitted grudgingly. "I've grown quite fond of you."

The unexpected declaration caught him completely by surprise, but more bewildering than the announcement was the way it made him feel. His heart lightened and a certain sense of manly satisfaction expanded in his chest, making him feel ridiculously—amazingly—happy.

It had been so long since he'd known true joy, the sensation almost knocked the breath out of him. She was a blip on the radar of his life, a passing thing, a fleeting character who would disappear from his world as soon as they located Theo... and yet her casual revelation left him with the certain impression that she was going to reverberate through his universe much longer than she'd be a part of it.

"You don't have to look so frightened," she teased, thankfully misreading his thoughts. "I'm fond of the bag boy at my local grocery store, too, and would probably try to save him, as well."

He feigned disappointment. "So I'm not special after all." He sighed.

She laughed at him. "Oh, please. If I did think you were special—me or any other woman, for that matter—you'd be gone faster than I could say commitment phobic," she said.

Intuitive, too, Will thought, though naturally he was going to argue with her. "So that's the quirk, is it? You're psychic?"

"No," she said. "But I am very good at...reading people." She lingered over the phrase, as though there were something significant that he was missing. His intuition flared.

"Reading people? How so? What do you mean?"

She sucked in a breath through her teeth, hesitating. "I already know how you're going to react," she said, more to herself than to him. "And you already think I'm weird."

"Not true. You're unique," he said, proving that he remembered her correction.

She chewed the corner of her lip, still seemingly undecided. She finally released a long breath and gave a what-the-hell shrug. "Have you ever heard of emotional intelligence?"

"Vaguely," he admitted, and a finger of unease nudged his belly.

"It's the science of learning to identify, control and manipulate the emotions of yourself and others. Learning to change harmful emotions into helpful ones." She tucked a leg under her bottom. "I actually teach a class on it at the local community college. Theo and I are keenly aware of other people's emotions, of what other people are feeling. When I was younger, I would just get…bombarded with feelings that didn't belong to me and I didn't know how to process them." Her troubled face was suddenly transformed with a soft smile. "Theo understood me—is probably the only person who ever has—and helped me learn how to cope with it."

The longer she'd talked the more tense he'd

become, and right now every muscle in his body felt as if it had atrophied. She could *feel* his emotions? All of them? The irritation, desire? God help him, the grief over what had happened? Did she feel that, too?

Help me...

Her ripe mouth curved into a knowing smile. "Relax," she said. "I haven't asked you a single question, have I?"

Yes, she had, Will thought. At the diner. When the crushing sadness had settled around him and he'd had to work a little harder to shrug it off. She'd put her hand on his, had asked him if he was okay.

He'd lied.

Hadn't he known there was something different about her? Hadn't the memories been worse since he'd met her, coming more and more frequently? Hadn't he been compelled to confide in her? He hadn't bared his soul, but he'd certainly been a hell of a lot more chatty with her than he'd ever been with anyone else. Her apparent ease with Mimi... It all made sense.

"Why don't you take a shower," she suggested. "Let the hot water work some of the knots out of your back."

He arched a brow, equally impressed by and terrified of her ability. It was intimidating to think that she knew his emotions, that she could feel them emanating from him. No secrets, stripped bare...

On the other hand, there was no point being coy about wanting her, Will decided.

She knew. No doubt had known all along.

"Reading my emotions?" he asked, lifting a brow again.

She chuckled. "Those, too, but your face is what's giving you away." Her eyes twinkled. "I've spooked you."

"It's...unnerving," he admitted, shooting her a look.

"It's not a cakewalk on this end, either," she said, grimacing significantly.

No, Will considered thoughtfully, he imagined not.

WELL, THAT HAD GONE about as well as she'd expected, Rhiannon thought later as she took her own shower. Will's scent still hung in the bathroom, flooding her senses and making that ever-present sense of longing curl tighter in her belly. Men were more careful of guarding their feelings than women were and any inkling of perceived weakness that went along with that was sure to rattle their cage.

Whatever Will was battling was substantial— she'd recognized that from the beginning. She'd felt

it the minute he'd made the connection—the trepi-
dation, the anxiety of her knowing that he wasn't
quite as together as he appeared. He wanted to be
in control, to govern his own thoughts and feelings,
and he damned sure didn't want to share them with
her.

No doubt he was waiting for her to ask what
had happened, what had made him leave a career
he'd obviously loved, what sort of horrific event
haunted his soul.

But she would not.

Feeling other people's emotions—things that
were private—was invasive enough. She would not
compound the unintentional intrusion by prying,
as well. Besides, she'd never had to pry. People
typically wanted to share with her. Provided they
had enough time, she suspected Will would, too.

And though she knew it was dangerous—that
any sort of emotional bonding with him would be
foolhardy—she wanted to know. She wanted to
soothe him. To try to help him heal. All of that
would simply invest her further into a relationship
she neither wanted nor needed—it was too close to
that unmanageable emotion known as love for her
liking. But she couldn't seem to help herself. Something about Will Forrester, other than his potent
sex appeal, called to her on a deeper, frighteningly
unfamiliar level.

Furthermore, though he had hadn't said as much, she'd felt his surprise that he'd told her about his parents and little brother. How terrible, she thought again. To lose your entire family in one fell swoop. Thankfully he'd had his grandparents and he seemed to hold them both in very high regard. Love and admiration had rung in his tone when he'd spoken of them, and she hadn't been kidding about getting spoiled with his courtesy.

Will Forrester was part of a dying breed—an authentic Southern gentleman. He said *please* and *thank you,* held open every door, including the car, and never failed to make her feel like anything but a lady...even when he was burning her up with one of those less than subtle I-want-to-fuck-you-blind looks.

It was thrillingly hot and made her equally so.

Even now, smelling his aftershave, knowing that he was in the other room—shirtless, a pair of low-slung shorts on—lying across the death bed made her nipples tingle and her sex quicken. Her belly clenched and an indecent throb built between her thighs.

Rhiannon turned off the shower, snagged a towel and quickly went through her evening routine. She moisturized, she partially dried her hair—it would take too long to do it properly and she didn't have the patience—then slipped into a pair of cotton shorts and matching cami.

Then she brushed her teeth.

Two minutes later she strolled back into their room and stowed her things. She felt Will's brooding gaze linger over her breasts, skim over her hips and settle on her ass, caressing her with the heat of that heavy-lidded stare. She could feel his desire— it was practically arcing off him, sparking against her own. In a minute, if she had her way, they were going to blaze out of control.

A dry bark of laughter rumbled from his chest. "Just out of curiosity, can you feel what I'm feeling now?"

She bent over—purposely allowing her shorts to ride up—and stowed her cosmetics bag in her suitcase.

She straightened slowly, then turned and looked at him. "I can," she admitted. "But not for the reasons you think."

He laced his fingers behind his head, doing his own little torture trick as his abs rippled invitingly. "I'm afraid I don't follow."

She sidled forward. "Luckily this isn't an intelligence test."

Another sexy laugh. "Explain, please."

Rhiannon sat on the edge of his bed and slid a finger deliberately down his belly. His unsteady breath hissed between his teeth, making her smile. "My feelings mirror your own, so they're sort of… tangled up. I can't tell which feelings are yours or which feelings are mine. I'm just doubly—" she bent forward and put her mouth a hairbreadth from his "—hot," she breathed.

She drew back and quirked a brow. "Well?" she asked.

Will's silvery-gray eyes darkened into a magnetic pewter shade and the grin that pulled at his lips was quite possibly the sexiest thing she'd ever seen. "You tell me," he said. "I bought a tube of your brand this morning, too."

Before she could laugh, he flipped her onto her back and his mouth was on hers. Hot, warm and demanding, his lips moved masterfully over her own. His tongue tangled around hers, probed the soft inner recesses of her mouth.

Her blood suddenly felt as if it was boiling and moving too damned slowly through her veins. She wriggled closer, thankful that he hadn't bothered with a shirt. His skin was smooth and sleek, supple muscle and perfect bone. She slid her palms over his shoulders, up into his hair and arched against him, gasping as the feel of her sensitive breasts met the weight of his chest. His shorn locks tickled her palms and she felt the long, hard length of him against her thigh.

Warmth abruptly pooled in her center and the throb she'd felt earlier pulsed with every quickened beat of her heart. Her breath came in desperate puffs and the overwhelming need to feel him inside her—to feel him pushing in and out, filling her up and laying her bare—all but obliterated every other sensation. She was a slave to the desire, a prisoner of the longing. The room could crumble into ruin around them and as long as he and the bed remained, she'd be fine.

She'd never felt this sort of intensity before, this absolute single-minded drive to have a man inside her. It was new and wondrous and just a little bit frightening, but the fear heightened the experience. She shifted, opening her legs, and gasped as he settled against her.

Rhiannon felt her eyes roll back in her head and a shaky, euphoric laugh rattled her chest. "Oh, sweet heaven," she said, pulling her thighs back and anchoring them around his waist. "This will be *so* much better when we're naked."

9

FOR ONCE THEY WERE in agreement, Will thought as Rhiannon's greedy thighs clamped around his hips. Her impatient hands slid over his back, down his ass and gave a determined squeeze, which sent him flexing against her once more. She bucked beneath him, not the least bit shy about what she wanted.

Him.

The knowledge almost set him off and he hadn't even fully had her yet.

He would.

He was going to map her body with his tongue, read her like Braille. He was going to fill his mouth with her pouting breasts and feast on her sweet sex until she came.

Then he was going to make her come again.

He left her mouth and licked a path down her

throat, savoring the taste of her on his tongue. She was sweet and tangy and he wanted to bury himself so far inside her that it would take some sort of nuclear weapon to blast him out.

Need hammered through his veins, blotting out everything to the exclusion of her. She was all he wanted. She was all that mattered. He found the crown of her breast through her shirt and suckled, and her little gasping purr of pleasure made him harden even more.

"You have been driving me crazy," he told her, slipping the straps of her shirt aside. Ah, perfect, Will thought. Heavy globes, rosy nipples puckered for his kiss. He laved her first, sampling, then suckled deep, giving a sharper tug.

Her breath hissed out of her mouth and she shifted her hips more provocatively against him. She bent forward and nipped at his shoulder, then licked a determined path up his neck and sighed hotly into his ear.

"Likewise," she said. "And you thought I was crazy before."

He smiled against her. "No, I didn't."

"Liar." She laughed, slipping a hand over his hip. She shifted and cupped him through his boxers, making what was left of his breath completely flee.

Small, capable hand stroking his dick, a sweet,

perky breast in his mouth and a woman who was clearly an uninhibited, enthusiastic bed partner beneath him.

Life could not possibly get any better.

Unless…

He dragged her little shorts off and was pleasantly surprised. "No panties?"

"You're gonna talk during sex, too? There are *so* many better things you could be doing with your mouth," she said, slipping a finger along the engorged head of his penis. A single bead of moisture leaked from the top and she swirled it around him with her thumb in a mind-numbingly distracting little circle.

"Like w-what?"

"Later," she said enigmatically. "When we have more time." She bucked against him. "Right now I want you to take me."

He had never in his life had a woman say that to him before, had always thought it was something that happened only in porn movies. But the fact that this woman had just said it to him made him absolutely want to beat his chest and roar. It was direct and sexy and, dammit, fucking fabulous, and he'd never—*never*—wanted another woman more.

Thankful that he'd had the forethought to buy the condoms when he'd gotten the new toothpaste, he snagged one from beneath the phone book, where he'd hidden it earlier, and quickly tore into it with his teeth.

She saw it and laughed. "Confident, were you?"

"Hopeful," he corrected as she dragged his boxers over his ass.

Her eyes darkened to a midnight-blue as she feasted her gaze on him. She licked her lips and took the protection from his hand. "Let me," she said.

A second later he was fully sheathed in the condom and a mere half a second after that, fully sheathed in her. He took her hard, plunging into her heat, and the gratified smile that slid over her lips as he finally filled her up triggered his inner caveman. His lips peeled away from his teeth as he pushed into her, harder and harder, almost savagely, and the more firmly he seated himself, the more she seemed to like it. Little grunts and groans of pleasure slipped past her carnal smile, and she raked her nails lightly over his back and gripped his ass. She drew her legs back, anchoring them around his waist, and met him thrust for thrust.

The headboard banged repeatedly against the wall and, while he knew the hotel was full and they were surely disturbing someone on the other side, he didn't give a damn.

Couldn't.

Her greedy muscles tightened around him with every thrust, holding him in, causing an exquisite draw and drag between their joined bodies. It was hot and hard and dirty, with an elemental primal intensity to it that made it hands down the best sex he'd ever had in his life.

And he hadn't even come yet.

But he was about to.

Could feel it building in his loins, gathering force as his balls tightened and the urgent, insistent tingle built in the root of his dick.

A little laugh tittered out of her throat, her eyes fluttered shut and then she suddenly went wild beneath him. Everything seemed to tighten around him—her legs, her arms, her sex. She bucked beneath him, forcing him to up the tempo.

"You are— Holy hell— I'm— *Damn*."

She went rigid beneath him as the orgasm took her. Her mouth opened in a long soundless scream that suddenly became a long, low moan of pleasure. Her toes curled into his ass and for whatever reason, that was what set him off.

The climax blasted from his loins like a bullet down the barrel of a gun and with every greedy squeeze of her body around him, another wave of sensation shuddered through him, milking his body of all it had left. Wringing him dry. He angled deep and seated himself as firmly into her as possible, felt his back bow beneath the stress of the pleasure and heard his own strangled cry in his ears.

Breathing hard, he lowered his head and looked down at her. Her wild dark curls were fanned out on the muted gold tones of the bedspread, her cheeks were flushed, her lips plump and swollen and her eyes knocked the breath out of him. She was wantonly beautiful, unrepentantly sexy, and the satisfied smile curling her mouth made him feel as if he'd conquered the world.

Or at the very least, hers.

She slid her hands over his back, tracing his spine with the tip of her nails. It felt delicious. "We're going to have to do that again."

He was still inside her, he could still feel her fisting around him and she was already game for more?

Crazy, unique, weird, odd…whatever.

She was officially perfect.

"So I'M GOOD ENOUGH to sleep with, but not good enough to sleep with?" Will teased the next morning when Rhiannon, still satisfied and drowsy, opened her eyes. He sat on the edge of his bed. He wore navy blue boxers—no shirt, amen—and an endearingly sexy smile.

She stretched and let go a long groan. "I thrash

around a lot," she lied, not wanting to hurt his feelings. She'd deliberately waited until his breathing was slow and deep and she was certain he was asleep before getting up and sneaking back to her own bed.

He inspected her bed, which was curiously undisturbed, and merely arched a brow. "I'm going to take a quick shower," he said. "Do you need it first?"

She shook her head. *Always polite,* she thought as he headed for the bathroom. A conscientious worker, a fabulous lover. Were she in the market for a permanent sort of man, he would definitely be a contender.

But she wasn't, Rhiannon reminded herself, and ignored the unwanted sense of melancholy that accompanied the thought.

Permanent went hand in hand with love and she'd decided long ago that she didn't want any part of that weakening, unpredictable emotion. She'd seen the damage it could do.

No, thank you.

And she was happy, dammit. Content.

So why had she wanted to linger long after the sex was over? Something she'd never had any desire to do before. Why had she wanted to feel his arm snugly around her middle, his breath in her ear, and why had it been so damned hard to leave his warm, curiously comfortable side and get into her own cold, lonely bed?

Better still, why did her bed feel lonely, when it never had before?

Quicksand, Rhiannon thought. If she wasn't careful, she could so easily sink.

The minute she'd felt her reluctance to move away from him, she'd made herself do it just to prove that she could. That he really wasn't different. She sighed.

But she knew he was.

Off-the-charts, otherworldly attraction aside, something about him made her simply go all gooey on the inside. He was smart and funny, interesting and wounded. And he was good, Rhiannon decided. If there was one thing she'd learned with her ability to read emotions over the years, she'd learned to be a good judge of character. So often people's emotions were tied to their motivations. After a while it was simple to pick up on false concern, a greedy heart, a malicious spirit. Will had none of those things.

He was unequivocally…honorable.

The adjective seemed out of date and old-fashioned, but it fit him all the same.

And right now he was doing all he could to survive, to put his world back together. She could feel the desperation behind the determination, could sense the ever-heavier cloak of grief, guilt and despair tightening around him. And she could just as easily feel him pushing against it, resisting it.

This was not her problem, Rhiannon knew, yet she longed to help him. To ease a bit of his burden. Unfortunately, she knew her assistance would not be welcomed. Because Will still believed he was fine.

The truth was coming, though, whether he wanted to face it or not.

The only thing that remained to be seen was whether they would still be together when that reckoning came.

Probably not, she thought, and her spirits sank like a spent party balloon.

Ridiculous, she countered, sitting up. She was a believer in EI. She would just not permit herself to feel this way. She crossed her legs and concentrated on getting her emotions under control, into channeling them into a healthier, prudent direction.

Will chose that moment to stroll out of the bathroom.

"Sorry," he said. "I didn't realize you were praying."

Her lips twitched. "I'm not praying right now," she said. "I'm...working on something."

"It looks unpleasant."

She kept her eyes closed, but still grinned.

"Could you shut up, please? You're interfering with my focus." Oh, who was she kidding? He'd blown it all to hell and back.

She felt him approach, and his soft breath drifted over her face. Oranges and cloves. "I actually like this toothpaste," he whispered. "You've converted me, and I'm brand loyal. You should be proud of yourself."

She opened her eyes. "And how much of your conversion is directly related to wanting to kiss me again?"

His eyes twinkled and dropped to her mouth. "A significant part."

"And will you go back to your minty toothpaste when I am no longer around?"

"Possibly."

"Traitor."

He kissed the tip of her nose, causing an unexpected rush of emotion coursing through her. "You wound me."

She harrumphed under her breath. "You are so full of shit."

"That's what I like about you," he said. "You're so careful with your opinions. Such a delicate little flower."

An image of her riding him for all she was worth suddenly materialized in her mind's eye and her stomach involuntarily tightened with longing at the reminder.

Hot, warm skin. Gleaming muscles. The feel of him buried deep inside her. His knuckle pressing against her clit as his mouth fed at her breasts.

He didn't treat her like a delicate little flower, thank God. He treated her as if he couldn't control himself, as if he couldn't take her hard enough, fast enough or completely enough. It made her feel wanted and feminine and womanly. She loved the way he suckled deeply from her breasts, not only taking her nipple into his mouth, but as much of the globe as he could, as well. As if he couldn't taste enough of her. It was raw and uninhibited and surpassed anything she'd ever experienced.

"I hate to rush you," he said. "But we should probably get moving. We've got a lot of ground to cover today."

Thankful for the subject change, Rhiannon reluctantly stood and stretched. "Has Tad even checked in?" she asked. She'd heard Will on the phone with Payne last night, but hadn't caught much of the conversation.

Will grimaced. "No. However, per our employment contract, he has been apprised of what we're doing."

She toyed with a strand of her hair. "Does he know I'm with you?"

"No."

"Good," she said, gathering her toiletries. She rolled her eyes. "You heard that ignorant message. The moron would assume that I was simply trying to help find Theo to further our reconciliation."

"You know you want him," Will teased.

"The hell you say," she shot back, feigning offense. "He's an ass."

He slid into a pair of worn denim jeans, but didn't bother to zip or button the snap while he looked for a shirt. Effortlessly sexy, she thought, her gaze tracing the fine line of hair that disappeared beneath the waist of his shorts. "But there has to be somebody, right?" he asked.

The question was casual, but she sensed more than curiosity behind it. She purposely kept her voice light. "No, there isn't. I'm happy with the status quo."

Her answer seemed to surprise him. "Really?"

She nodded once. "Really." That ought to put to rest any lingering fears that she would become clingy. "What about you?" she asked just as lightly, though his answer was ridiculously important to her. "Any girl waiting for you back home in—" She frowned. "Where did you say you were from originally?"

He shrugged into his trademark black T-shirt. "Mockingbird, Mississippi," he told her. "And no."

His gaze tangled with hers. "I, too, am happy with the status quo."

"No ring, then?" she asked, snapping her fingers with feigned regret.

He merely laughed.

"Where is Mockingbird, Mississippi?" She wanted to know. It sounded quaint, much like Begonia.

"Heart of the Delta," he said. "Two traffic lights, one grocery store and ten churches." He flashed a grin. "Much like any small Southern town."

He'd certainly nailed that. "And your grandmother is still there?"

"She is." He zipped his suitcase and set it on the floor, then collected his laptop bag.

"What's her name?" Names were important. She could always conjure a face to go with a name, even if it was wrong.

"Molly."

Dark hair and eyes, a plump face and a smile that was kind and slightly mischievous, Rhiannon thought, instantly picturing his grandmother.

"Any other relatives?"

He sighed. "Just the assorted aunts, uncles and cousins I only see every few years."

Sounded like her. And she actually lived close to most of her family.

"What about you? Surely you're not in Begonia all alone."

"Not exactly," she said, gathering her outfit for the day. "My parents are in Florida and are regulars at Disney World. They do their part to contribute to the local economy."

He chuckled. "That's admirable. What about the rest of your family?"

She sighed. "Like you, they're scattered around town, but I rarely see them. We're not close." She frowned. "Theo is really the closest thing to family that I have, and I chose him."

"He's lucky," Will said, surprising her with the sincere comment. Something shifted behind his eyes, but it was gone before she could make an identification.

"We both are."

She jerked her hand toward the bathroom. "Speaking of which, I should probably hurry." She gathered her things. "I'll only be a minute."

"I'll time you."

She laughed. "Two, then."

"You've got ninety seconds."

"Kiss my ass."

"I'm willing to adjust our schedule if you really mean it," he said silkily.

His voice sent a shiver of longing through her that settled warmly in her womb.

She was so, *so* in over her head, Rhiannon thought. And simply drowning no longer seemed like such a bad alternative.

10

WEAVING THROUGH the libraries and cemeteries around Roanoke was long, tedious work and at the end of the day, other than being able to cross several smaller towns and half a dozen libraries off their list, they had little to show for it.

The strain, he could tell, was beginning to get to Rhiannon. There was a new tightness around her eyes and, though she was still the same charmingly strange, smart-assed girl he'd come to know over the past few days, there was a hollowness to her laughter that hadn't been there before.

She genuinely loved Theo Watson and, though Will didn't want her to love him—he was rebuilding his life right now and didn't have time for anything other than fleeting companionship—he was suddenly more envious of that old man than he'd ever been of anybody.

It completely defied logic, and he'd been trying all day to convince himself that it wasn't true, but Will grimly suspected he knew better. He envied Theo her unconditional affection. He envied him that place in her life. He envied him the right to enjoy her company.

Refreshingly, he hadn't even had to make the disclaimer to Rhiannon, because he knew she was only interested in the same thing.

So why had he asked her if there was a guy in the picture? Will wondered. And why had his guts twisted and hadn't released until she said no? Honestly, what was it about her, specifically, that had gotten him all snarled up in knots?

Furthermore, why had he felt a thrill of a challenge flare in his belly when she'd quite plainly let him know that she was happy with her status quo? He was happy, too, and yet he wanted to be her exception to the rule. He inwardly snorted.

He was acting like a chick, he realized, and the knowledge promptly soured on his tongue.

She was seriously knocking him off his game, Will thought, one he grimly suspected he might end up losing.

And then there was the other issue, the one he'd been trying not to think about, the galling knowledge that she could feel the pressing weight of regret that shadowed his every move…and it was only getting worse. Will had thought that leaving the military would help, that the distance would do him good, and to some degree he'd been right.

Unfortunately he'd walked right out of that nightmare into one with a woman who seemed to be some sort of emotional astringent, and every minute he spent with her—every sexually satisfying, curiously enjoyable second—he could feel himself losing ground, could feel everything he'd managed to keep locked down boiling up inside him.

Skinny, scabbed knees, Spider-Man T-shirt and blood. So much blood...

He squeezed his eyes tightly shut and beat the images away, replacing them with her smiling face, the way she'd sunk her teeth into her bottom lip as he'd plunged into her, that little grin she'd worn when she'd smelled those flowers last night. Happy snapshots of memory, and he realized too late the significance that they were all of her.

Shit.

Presently they were sitting in another dingy back room in another tiny library, flipping a page at a time through the microfiche records. The little octogenarian in charge with a pack-a-day voice had let them know in no uncertain terms that she would close promptly at five and all records had to be returned to their proper place. She'd checked on them a few minutes ago and had told them that she was stepping out back to have a smoke. Big surprise there. They had fifteen minutes.

Rhiannon closed the final file, returned it to its slot and sighed as her shoulders sagged.

"Another dead end," she said. "This is going to take forever."

"Not forever," Will corrected. "But it is going to take time."

Frustration laced her tired voice. "Don't you feel like we're running out of that?"

"Not at all," he said. "We're actually making good progress, better than Theo, I'd wager. We *will* find him. I am certain of that."

"I wish I was as optimistic," she said, leaning her head against his shoulder. The innocuous gesture smacked of familiarity and trust, things he wasn't accustomed to feeling with a woman, and naturally, burned through him like a wildfire. He had tried to act like a professional today—he *was* working, after all—but it had been damned hard.

All of him, he thought darkly.

For what felt like the thousandth time today, he wondered if his "relationship," for lack of a better term, with Rhiannon would get him fired. He wasn't altogether sure that they'd sack him for it, but he could hardly blame them if they did. He sincerely doubted screwing around with someone directly involved in his *first* case—he resisted the pressing urge to snort—was considered good form. He'd intimated as much to Payne, though, and the man had still advised him to take her along. Of course, Payne probably thought he had enough sense of restraint and self-preservation to resist her.

His gaze slid to her once more—the elfin face, that especially cute little nose and lush, pink mouth. His dick stirred, readying for sport.

Clearly he did not.

He turned and wrapped his arms around her, meaning to simply comfort her. That was all. He could control himself, he thought, even as her soft body melded against his as though it had been made especially for his arms.

Comforting her worked for a moment, then he felt her lips on his throat and soothing her suddenly was no longer his primary objective.

Getting into her again was.

It was madness, sheer and utter insanity, but he couldn't seem to help himself…and didn't want to.

Without the slightest bit of hesitation, he found her lips and breathed a sigh of relief into her mouth when he tasted her again. She made him crazy. Absolutely wrecked him. A need that was never fully sated reared up at the slightest provocation and pulled him under. His muscles tensed, his loins burst into flame and the desire to plant himself between her thighs again obliterated every other thought.

It didn't matter that they were in a tiny little library in the middle of nowhere with a librarian who was more a warden than a book lover. It didn't matter that he could potentially lose his job—he was damned either way now anyway, right? Sinner or saint, he was still going to hang.

He just wanted her. God help him, had to have her.

"I can't keep my hands off you," she confessed, as though it were a mortifying weakness.

"Good," he said, setting her on the table, thankful that she'd worn another skirt. He freed himself and pulled a condom from his pocket, then swiftly rolled it into place. "I like it when your hands are on me."

He nudged her gratifyingly damp panties aside, then he pushed into her and his world fell back into place. Everything settled into its rightful position and the breath he'd been holding leaked out of his lungs in a sigh of relief that felt dredged from his very soul.

He rested his forehead against hers and smiled, silently admitting to himself that he was doomed.

She sighed, as well, as though she needed him as much as he needed her, then scooted forward, wrapping her legs around his waist and her arms around his neck.

"Take me," she said once again, his own personal porn star.

And he did.

THE DESPAIR and frustration she'd felt only seconds ago seemed like a distant memory, Rhiannon thought now as Will's big warm hands settled on her hips and he pushed into her.

She sighed, savoring the sensation, and clamped her feminine muscles around him. He was hot and hard and completely filled her up, chasing away an emptiness she hadn't known existed, would have sworn she'd never felt.

She wrapped her hands around his neck and held on as he repeatedly plunged into her, in and out, in and out, harder and faster. Her breath came in labored little puffs and her nipples tingled with every thrust of his body into hers.

"I've been thinking about this all day," she confessed. "Wanting you all day."

And it was true. Every cell in her body had been keenly aware of him, practically singing with his nearness. She'd looked at his mouth and gone wet, let her gaze linger on the smooth column of his throat and something in her belly had gone all hot and muddled.

And his hands...

Damn, how she loved his hands. Big, capable, wonderful on her body. They made her feel small and feminine, safe and protected, enflamed and unbelievably alive.

He smiled down at her and nuzzled her ear with his nose, sending a wave of gooseflesh racing down her spine. "You could have said something. It's been hell keeping my hands off you."

"I was...trying to be...good," she said, leaning back so that he could get better access. She shifted forward, aligning their bodies so that she could feel his balls slapping against her sensitized flesh.

It felt *wonderful*. Positively wicked.

She bit her bottom lip as pleasure bolted through her, felt her neck grow weak and her head heavy. The flash of climax ripened in her womb, building and building, growing heavier and more insistent with every frenzied stroke of him deep inside her.

"I like it when you're bad," he told her. "It's sexy."

"I was waiting on you to snap," she said. "Your control is impressive."

And it was true. She'd been trying to make him crack all day. Little touches, a heavy-lidded look, double entendres left and right, and yet he'd determinedly clung to his self-control. It was infuriating. She'd wanted to make him give in first today—for reasons she'd couldn't begin to fathom, that had seemed vitally important—and then he'd wrapped his arms around her and the affection she'd felt in the gesture had been equally bittersweet and terrifying.

Affection wasn't supposed to be a part of this, and worse still, she wasn't supposed to want it.

And then, because she'd needed a distraction—a reminder of what they were supposed to be, that this was casual and nothing more—she'd given in and kissed his neck, knowing that it would set him off.

He chuckled. "You weren't the only one trying to be good," he confessed. "I *am* supposed to be working."

Her gaze tangled with his. "By law you're supposed to get a fifteen-minute break every four hours." She felt a cry of pleasure build in her throat and swallowed it back. She fisted around him, holding him to her. "You're good."

Something in his expression changed, his eyes smoldered and, without warning, he lifted her off the table and backed her against the wall. The shift in her weight and their positions was absolutely eyes-rolling-back-in-her-head perfect.

She gasped as he managed to hit a hidden spot deep within her, nailing the supersensitive flesh with each brutal thrust into her body. She wrapped her legs tighter around his waist and, catching his rhythm, worked herself up and down on him. She tasted his neck, slid her fingers into his hair and gave a little tug. He growled low in his throat and pounded harder, pushing into her with relentless, reckless force. Knickknacks on a shelf wobbled ominously and the sound of her ass and back hitting the wall reverberated like a gunshot repeatedly through the room. She was breathing too loudly, making too much noise, and she buried her face in his shoulder in an attempt to drown out her own cries.

"Come for me," he said.

And she did. On command. The orgasm broke over her with enough force to make her spine go rigid. Sparklers danced behind her lids and her vision blackened around the edges. She couldn't catch her breath and then stopped trying—oxygen seemed overrated at the moment compared to the cataclysmic storm of sensation whirling through her sex. She fisted around him and with every forceful spasm, another almost unbearable bolt of feeling swept through her.

Will pistoned in and out of her, pounded into her as though he couldn't take her hard enough—rough and thrilling, elemental and raw—and little masculine growls of pleasure slipped between his clenched teeth.

Her orgasm seemed to trigger his own and he suddenly shuddered against her, angling high and burying deep, seating himself as far into her as he could. A low, purely masculine cry stuttered out of his mouth and his hands tightened against her rump, holding her utterly still as the force of his release rocketed through him. She could feel him pulsing inside her, sending another shudder of sensation racking through her.

Breathing hard, spent and fully sated, Rhiannon pressed a kiss to his temple. "You need to be bad more often," she said.

He grinned. "Likewise."

A bell tinkled in the distance and her eyes widened as that significant sound registered in her foggy brain.

Will chuckled. "Can you stand?"

She nodded, not altogether sure that was true. "If not, I'll just lean here," she said. "And try to look normal."

He carefully set her down, snagged a tissue from a nearby box on the table—evidently dust was a problem in this airless little room, she thought—and quickly disposed of the condom.

When she was sure her legs wouldn't give way,

Rhiannon pushed tentatively away from the wall and dragged her skirt back down over her hips into its proper position. Meanwhile Will tucked his shirt back in and zipped his pants. They were presentable, she realized, but the scent of sex hung heavy in the air, betraying their latest activity. Rather than have the librarian wander in and assess the situation, she quickly grabbed her purse and his hand and darted from the room.

Just in time, too. Mrs. Marcus was on her way back. "I'm closing," she announced without preamble. She smelled like menthol and mint, and the scent instantly triggered Rhiannon's gag reflex. "If you didn't find what you were looking for, you can come back tomorrow. We open at nine."

"Thank you," Will murmured, nodding his goodbye—ever the gentleman, Rhiannon thought.

She covered her mouth, gagging again, and he quickly propelled her out the door, quiet laughter shaking his shoulders. "Are you okay?"

Rhiannon pulled a cleansing breath into her nose and glared at him reprovingly. "Yes," she said. "Don't make fun. I told you I can't stand it. Ugh. That was strong. My nose is still burning."

He still chuckled. "Minty breath, your Achilles' heel." He threaded his fingers through hers and tugged her toward the Jeep. "You got any other quirks I should know about? Anything else that might make for an awkward situation?" He opened the door for her and waited for her to climb in.

She pretended to think. "I cry during credit-card commercials, I'm afraid of clowns and spiders, I am anti-pumpkin pie and am Begonia's current watermelon-seed-spitting champion." She paused and slid him a look. "I have no desire to be spanked, but a little light bondage sounds intriguing."

His eyes glazed over comically and she laughed. "You okay?"

He determinedly closed her door and joined her in the car in record time, then cranked the engine and quickly darted out onto the highway. "In a hurry?" she asked, unable to hide her grin. "Where are we going?"

He tapped his thumb against the steering wheel and slid her a smoldering look. "To a hardware store. We're going to need some rope."

11

"So you're afraid of clowns?" Will asked, taking a draw from his beer. They'd found another hotel for the night—the same chain that had suited her before—and had settled in at a little Irish pub. The music wasn't too loud, the beer was cold and the food was delicious. His gaze slid over Rhiannon.

And naturally, the company was above par.

She sipped her whiskey—Jameson, so he had to approve—and her eyes twinkled with warmth. "*And* I'm the watermelon-seed-spitting champion," she reminded him. "I thought you'd be impressed with that. I beat out several men for that auspicious title."

There were lots of things that about her that impressed him, but that didn't necessarily make his list. Still…

He nodded, chasing a bead of moisture down

the side of his bottle with his finger. "You're an impressive woman."

She rolled her eyes. "You thought I was crazy."

"I never said that," he told her.

She tapped her temple. "Didn't have to, remember?"

He thought about lying, but no doubt she would pick up on that, too. "I thought you were...different," he admitted, somewhat reluctantly.

She laughed, the sound hearty and uninhibited, much like her. "That's a politically correct description if I've ever heard one."

He took another drink. "More diplomatic, I would say."

Her dark blue gaze caught his and she seemed to be considering something. "Actually, it was the gentlemanly response." She tipped her glass at him. "I like that about you. It's refreshing."

So she'd said, Will thought as another one of those increasing urges to bare his soul whisked through him. His hand tightened around his bottle and he determinedly beat it back.

She grinned and quirked a knowing brow, but didn't ask. She never asked, and after a moment he wondered why. He knew she had to be curious, had to wonder what haunted him.

"What?" he asked. "No questions? You're just

going to arch your sleek little brow and give me that I-know-your-secrets look?"

"I don't know your secrets," she said. "I only know the pain."

Her expression grew thoughtful and she seemed to focus on something he couldn't see. It made him unaccountably nervous and he belatedly wished he'd kept his thoughts to himself.

"Regret," she murmured. "Loss. Shame. And something else," she said, her gaze tangling with his once more. "Something elusive that I can't put my finger on."

More disturbed by her assessment than he could ever have imagined, Will felt an uncomfortable laugh rattle out of his throat. "Well, if you can't figure it out, I'll be damned before I try."

She hesitated again, then leaned forward, drawing him in once again. He could feel his center of gravity shift, inexplicably pulling him closer to her. "The feeling of someone else's private emotions is intrusive enough," she said. "I can't help it, but it doesn't negate my accountability. So stop worrying that I'm going to ask you about it. I have my suspicions, of course." Her lips twisted. "I've been me for a long time, you know, and there are certain markers for particular emotions." She reached across the table and laid her hand on his. As always, her touch sent his heart into an irregular rhythm and sizzled through him. "But I will not add insult to injury by asking you to explain it to me."

Wow, Will thought, impressed by her compassion and conscience. She was...simply remarkable. If he were as emotionally attuned to other people, would he be so magnanimous? he wondered. Would he resist the urge to mine those emotions and the impulse to interfere?

He cleared his throat, uncertain what to say. "Thank you," he finally murmured.

"Thank Theo," she said, leaning back once more. "I didn't used to always be so sensitive."

He chuckled. That fit, actually. It was the logical, compassionate response to her gift. He could see her wanting to help, to soothe. It was her nature, after all.

She folded the edges of her napkin. "I didn't used to appreciate the fact that just because I could pick up on a person's emotions it didn't mean that I *owned* them. I had no claim to them, though I felt them, as well."

He studied her. "Sounds like that would be confusing."

"It was, in the beginning." She blew out a breath. "But like I said, Theo helped me. He is much more empathetic than I am. He can pick up on subtle nuances I can't even detect."

"I imagine that's more curse than blessing," Will remarked.

She merely smiled. "It comes in handy."

He grinned, but it faltered. "So you said you had your suspicions," he stated in a leading way.

Her expression grew cautiously still. "I do. Are you asking me to share them?"

"I'm curious as to how close to the mark you are," he murmured.

She considered him another minute, testing the atmosphere around him, he imagined. "All right, then," she said. "The weight I feel around you... It's enormously heavy. The grief, the shame and the regret feel like death to me, like you blame yourself for it."

He locked every muscle in his body to stem the shudder trying to break through him and she must have felt that, too, because she suddenly reached across the table and took his hand again. Her smile was sad.

"When I consider the fact that you were a Ranger—underwent all that training to achieve the goal—then that tells me you had planned to make a full career out of the military. That you never intended to leave. You're focused, driven and loyal. Quitting would never have been a part of your plan."

He gave a little breath and smiled at her insight.

"Which means you lost someone close to you—a comrade, maybe?"

The silence lengthened between them as Will struggled to block the images her stunningly accurate words conjured. *Crumpled little bodies, slain women, and the boy...*

The one he'd tried to save, but hadn't been able to.

Help me...

Blood was a common enough occurrence on the battlefield, but he couldn't seem to get the stench of that child's out of his nose no matter how hard he tried. He stared at his beer, followed a flurry of bubbles up the side of the bottle and gave his head a small shake.

"Frightening close," he finally admitted to her, tightening his hand around his drink to hide the shake.

She winced with regret. "I'm sorry."

"Bad intel," he told her, the words welling up inside him. "Women and children." *Bloodied teddy bear, stained shirt.* "A boy. I...couldn't save him." And he'd felt that child take his last breath in his arms. The cloak of dread that had been stalking him for months suddenly settled over his shoulders and he couldn't shrug it off. It clung to him determinedly, tightened around his neck, making him feel as if he was choking. The grief, the despair, the failure. It hurt to feel it, and the pain made him feel weak. Irrational, he knew, but it didn't change anything.

Her hand squeezed his. "I'm so sorry," Rhiannon again said softly. "When you say bad intel...what does that mean? Your information was wrong?"

He tried to focus, struggled to find the words to explain. "Yeah," he murmured, remembering. "Insurgents were supposed to be in the area. They'd set a trap. Waited from a distance as we moved in, then remote detonated, you know?" Bastards, Will thought. "We retaliated, of course, and by the time we realized our enemy wasn't there...it was too late."

"And you feel responsible?"

"My team," he said. "I was point."

"And the people who died, the boy, you're certain it was your weapons that killed them?"

His lips twisted into a bitter, cynical smile. "Does it matter?"

She looked away and made a small face. "No, I guess it doesn't."

Once again the silence swelled between them and Will gave a shaky, hollow laugh. "You're good," he said. "Even the shrink couldn't get me to talk about this and yet you—" his gaze searched hers "—you don't even ask and I spill my guts."

Unreal, he thought. And like a boil being lanced, the relief was instantaneous. It still ached, the pain lingered, but the reprieve was nice. It wouldn't last, of course. He was a marked man—the experience had changed him. He'd never be able to fully let it go, but it would be nice to know he was going to be able to function.

She pulled a sheepish shrug. "I'm a magnet," she told him.

"A what?"

"That's not an official term, just my own," she said. "But I basically have that effect on people. I draw them out, so to speak. I always have. Total strangers have been known to spill their guts to me in the checkout lane and once during my pelvic exam my gynecologist told me that she was tired of her unattentive husband and was leaving him." She winked and tipped her beer into her mouth. "Interesting conversation."

Will chuckled and shook his head. A magnet, eh? That sure as hell made sense…because he'd be damned if he could stay away from her.

And he was quickly losing the will to try.

RHIANNON STARED at her reflection in the bathroom mirror in Madigan's Irish Pub and wished the little four-leaf clovers pressed behind the glass in the frame would truly bring good luck. She needed it right now.

She'd known that the grief Will had been carrying around was substantial—had felt that all along—and even though her suspicions had been damned close to the mark, having them confirmed in his stilted Southern drawl while the agony rolled off him in waves was almost more than she could bear.

Though she'd wanted to point out that this was not his fault—on any level—she instinctively knew that he would never completely relinquish ownership of the blame. It was still too fresh, the horror too vivid in his mind to even consider releasing any personal responsibility.

Does it matter? he'd said, with that heartbreakingly sad smile.

Ultimately, it did not, and Rhiannon knew in his place she would no doubt feel the same.

On the plus side—if there were a silver lining to this conversation—she'd felt the first vestiges of the gloom lift a bit off his shoulders and she desperately wanted to believe that she had played a key part in that. Helping him had become almost as important to her as finding Theo, and she hadn't realized that until she'd had to excuse herself to the bathroom where she could take a moment to simply weep.

For him.

Because she knew he wouldn't do it.

Finished now—she hoped, at any rate—she took a bracing breath and splashed a bit of cold water on her face. Her eyes were slightly puffy, her nose a bit red, but she would fake a sneeze when she returned to their table and tell him that the air freshener had set her off.

She took another deep breath and shook the tremors off her hands. Dammit, she had to get hold of herself. She was beginning to care too much, to feel too much when she was around him. Wonderful sex aside, there was a niggling feeling that she was sliding down a slippery slope and if she didn't dig her nails in now and cling to the side of the cliff, she'd fall right off into the murky unknown.

Love.

The very word sent a dart of panic right into her heart. Fickle, unpredictable, uncontrollable emotion. Made fools of smart people, made the strong weak and rendered all other emotions virtually useless. It was the trump card, the boss, and up until now she'd never been the least bit tempted to dip her pinkie toe into its vast pond.

And she wasn't now, Rhiannon tried to tell

herself, squeezing her eyes tightly shut. He was just an especially nice guy with great hands, who had the singular ability to unleash her baser instincts. He could draw an orgasm out of her faster than she could do it herself—which was saying something—and he made her want to climb right out of her skin and into his. Her heart fluttered with sweet anticipation and a strange sort of release when he kissed her, and her sex sang when he put those wonderfully large hands on her body. It was new and different, even special, she would concede.

But it wasn't love.

It couldn't be.

Will raised a brow in concern when she sat back down at their table, and she sighed.

"Damned air freshener in the bathroom," she complained with a beleaguered huff of annoyance. "As if we're not breathing enough chemicals in the air, let's add some that are pine scented."

He grinned. "Does pine make you gag, as well?"

"No, it makes me sneeze," she said, a bit through her nose for the proper effect.

He shook his head. "And to think I almost bought one of those little trees to hang from my rearview mirror." He *tsked.*

"And spoil your new-car smell? Blasphemous."

He looked at her plate. "Were you finished? You didn't eat much."

She'd lost her appetite during their discussion, but she couldn't very well tell him that. "It was a lot of food," she said. "I just couldn't finish it."

He didn't look convinced. "So you're ready, then?"

She nodded and reached to grab her purse. Madigan's was located a block off the little town square. "Why don't we take a walk?" she suggested. "Do a little window-shopping."

"It would have to be window-shopping," he said. "From the looks of things, they roll the streets up at five."

Will left enough money on the table to cover the bill and a generous tip, then stood. He literally towered over her. She'd noticed before, of course, but it never failed to send a thrill right to her midsection. Seemingly without thinking, he reached out and took her hand.

Feeling his against her own made her heart do that funny thing in her chest, but the rightness of his fingers threaded through hers quickly calmed her down. She wasn't used to being soothed, and had to admit the sensation was quite pleasant.

They walked past a five-and-dime, a beauty

parlor, a formal dress-wear shop, a shoe repair store—she hadn't seen one of those in a long time—various antiques stores and a little shop that boasted nothing but dollhouses and assorted accessories.

The only store still open was an ice cream parlor, and they ducked in and each got a scoop of pralines and cream in a waffle cone, then walked to the middle of the square and sank down on a park bench, where they could enjoy the fountain gurgling happily in front of them. It was twilight and the gas streetlamps sparkled to life, casting an orange glow. Kids zoomed along on their skateboards, ladies power walked in pairs and several people were taking their animals for their evening adventure.

Rhiannon sighed and licked her cone. "This is very Norman Rockwell," she said, giggling.

Will chuckled. "I keep waiting for Barney Fife to walk up and give us a citation for loitering."

She gasped delightedly. "I love Andy Griffith! I've got every season and special on DVD and am especially proud of my Fife Nip It in the Bud T-shirt."

He inspected his cone, looking for where it was melting the fastest. "You're joking."

"About what? The DVDs or the T-shirt?"

"The T-shirt," he said. "I'm with you on the DVDs, but the T-shirt is a no."

She rolled her eyes and snorted. "This coming from a man who wears the same T-shirt every day."

"It's not the same shirt. It's a clean version of the previous shirt."

"Yes, in black," she said. "Why don't you just print *Badass* in capital letters across the front? That would get the point across better." She took another swipe at her cone.

He leaned his head back and guffawed. "If you think I need a shirt to get that point across, then clearly I am not intimidating enough."

"You don't intimidate me at all," she told him, knowing that it was a lie. The things he made her feel scared the hell out of her and he damned sure didn't need a T-shirt for that.

Come to think of it, he was much more daunting when he was naked.

Another laugh sounded in her ear. "I'm not the least bit surprised about that. You don't scare me, either."

Ah…so she wasn't the only one who was lying, Rhiannon thought, feeling his sudden uneasiness. Because she'd lost any sort of perspective at all, she was almost giddy with the insight.

She nudged his shoulder. "I haven't tried to yet."

He slid her a wary glance. "Yet?"

She popped the last bit of ice cream cone into her mouth and smiled at him. "I'm going to scare the hell out of you tonight."

"How so?"

"With that length of rope we picked up at the hardware store today."

He stilled completely and a slow smile spread over his lips. "That's for you. You said you were intrigued by a little light bondage."

"Yes, but I never said *I* was the one who was going to be tied to the bed, did I?"

12

"THERE'S NO WAY IN HELL I'm letting you tie me to that bed," Will announced as Rhiannon twirled the length of rope in her hands.

Her face fell into a deliberate pout. "Damn," she said. "There were things I wanted to do." She waited a beat and then peeked up at him from beneath her lashes. "To you."

A cold sweat broke out across his shoulders at the innuendo and missed opportunity in her voice, but...*no*. She seriously couldn't expect to tie him up. He would readily own his control issues. He had them, he knew. And yet the promise of those things she'd wanted to do to him hung in the air between them, taunting him.

"One arm," he said, offering a compromise.

She shook her head. "Where's the fun in that? I want you completely at my mercy. I want to be able to explore and play and drive you crazy without fear of retribution." Another tragic sigh. "I wanted to be completely...uninhibited."

That was all it took to make him rock hard. She didn't so much as have to touch him. She didn't have to smile or let her eyes go all soft and wicked. She just had to make a few vague references and his dick acted as though she'd called it forward, her own devoted familiar.

He leveled his gaze at her, wavering. "You're not going to do anything terrible like leave me here for the hotel staff to find, or dress me in your underwear and take pictures and post them on the Internet, are you?"

Her lips curled into an indulgent smile. "Have you given me any reason to do that?"

"None that I can think of, no." But it still made him nervous. Surrendering control. As she'd said, being at her mercy.

She sidled forward and wrapped the rope sinuously around his wrist. "I promise you I won't do anything to you that you don't like." Her warm breath fanned against his arm. "I actually think you'll be pleasantly surprised."

Just like that, his will faltered. "In that case," he told her, holding out his arm, "bind me."

Her eyes twinkled. "You'll be my slave?"

He gloomily suspected he already was. "Yours to command."

"Then get naked."

He chuckled.

"And lie down."

He shucked his shorts and had the pleasure of watching her gaze droop in satisfaction. "And you have the nerve to say that I'm bossy?"

She grinned at him. "And shut up."

Minutes later he was sprawled across the bed, his arms stretched out over his head and securely fastened to the bedposts. A commingled sense of unease and anticipation made for a weird cocktail of sensation coursing through his blood. He couldn't believe that he'd let her talk him into this, that he'd actually allowed himself to be tied up. Though he trusted her not to do anything embarrassing or horrid to him, there was still the niggling inkling of being powerless, of being exposed.

Rhiannon stood at the foot of the bed and tapped her chin thoughtfully as she looked him over. Her gaze lingered on his dick and it instantly nodded a salute. A laugh that sounded dangerously hysterical erupted from his chest.

"Where to start?" she murmured. She shrugged out of her shirt, shucked her skirt—did the woman ever wear panties?—then coolly popped the front clasp of her lacy pink bra. The fabric sagged away from her breasts, catching on her nipples. With a casual lift of her shoulders, it fell off, leaving her just as bare and open as he was.

He felt marginally better.

"Would you like me to make a suggestion?" he asked.

"I thought I told you to be quiet." She crawled like a cat up along his body and rubbed her erect nipples across his chest. A hiss slipped beneath her teeth, straight into his blood.

"Ah," she said, letting her lids flutter shut. "Nice."

Without warning, she moved up and suckled his neck right beneath his jaw, then ran her hands down his chest and carefully slid her nails over his nipples.

Sensation bolted through him and he bucked slightly beneath her. He turned his head and kissed her neck, nipping her jawline, but before he could catch her mouth, she slid down his body, pausing to lick his chest, outline his ribs with her tongue and fingers, mapping every muscle, ridge and bone. Her hands kneaded him, insistent and greedy on his skin, and when her hair slid over the tops of his thighs he thought he was going to tear the posts away from the bed.

"Untie me," he said hoarsely. "I want to touch you. I need to touch you."

She took him in hand, then peeked up at him from between his legs. "Sorry," she said. "I'm busy." Then she deliberately took the whole of him into her mouth. There was no timid touching with the tip of her tongue, no tentative lick along the side of his dick.

She ate him.

And he'd never seen anything so profoundly sexy in his life.

Will's breath left in a startled whoosh and he groaned from deep in his throat. She sucked him, working the hot, slippery skin against her tongue, then wrapped her hand around him and used both to drive him crazy. In and out, up and down, a deliberate swirl of her tongue over his head, then she suckled the sensitive spot—unbeknownst to him—just below his head on the underside of his penis and he came dangerously close to coming right then.

"Rhiannon," he growled as the orgasm built force in his loins. "If you don't stop that, I'm going to—" She cupped his balls, took another long deep pull, simultaneously working her tongue against him, and he completely lost it. *"Come."* The word ripped from his throat as the release rocketed from his loins.

And just as if he was the ice cream cone he'd watched her eat earlier, she licked him up, savoring his essence on her tongue. If anything, she looked as if he tasted better, and the satisfaction of knowing that called to his inner caveman, made him want to drag her by the hair back to his cave and never let her go.

"Mmm." She sighed as she finished him off. "That was very good."

His laugh bordered on frantic.

"I hope you don't need a lot of downtime," she said as she slowly stroked him again. "Because I'm not finished with you yet."

He instantly hardened once more and shot her a self-satisfied smile. "I'm g-good," he told her, though it seemed like a vast understatement. He was *so* much better than good.

He was fucking fantastic.

Rhiannon snagged a condom and swiftly rolled it into place, then scaled his body once more. She winced with pleasure as the head of his dick bumped her clit and she slid back and forth along the ridge, coating him in her own juices. She was hot and wet and he set his jaw so hard he could have sworn he felt it crack.

His eyes almost rolled back in his head and once again the desire to touch her, to taste her breasts made him pull against his restraints. But something about the restriction heightened the experience. She set the pace. She was in control.

And she was brilliant at it.

Her dark hair slithered around her shoulders, down over her breasts, playing hide-and-seek with her nipples. Her lips, soft pink and swollen, rose in a sensual half smile and the dark thatch of hair between her thighs as it rested over him was quite possibly the most incredible thing he'd ever seen.

Gorgeous, he thought, thunderstruck with awe.

She lifted her hips and then slowly sank onto him, her breath leaking out in a long, slow hiss as though his invasion into her body was somehow pushing it out of her. Her heat completely engulfed him. He instinctively flexed beneath her, pushing up.

The slight movement made her grin and she rocked forward on him again, up and down, up and down, then bent forward and laved his nipple with her tongue while clamping tightly around him. *Who knew?* he thought as a flash fire flared down his middle and landed in his groin.

She leaned back once more, her hands on his chest, and she rode him hard. His arms strained against the bindings as he pushed up into her, bucking to meet her downward thrusts. A low purr built in the back of her throat and he watched her face as she caught the first spark of climax. She chased it, her hips undulating wildly against him, then she reached down and massaged her clit. A mere sweep of her fingers sent her flying over the edge and a low, keening cry ripped from her lungs.

She tightened hard around him, triggering his own release, and though he wouldn't have thought it possible, this orgasm was even more powerful than the last. He bucked and shuddered beneath her, every muscle clenched and spent.

Rhiannon collapsed on top of him, boneless and sated, and he felt her lips press a tender kiss against his chest.

It was that kiss—that small gesture—that propelled him over the edge of reason, and he felt himself fall, quite irrationally and against his better judgment, in love with her.

"ARE YOU GOING TO LET ME GO NOW?" Will wanted to know as she curled up against his chest.

She smiled against him. "I thought you were my slave."

"Yes, but even love slaves need to attend to necessary business."

"Damn." She sighed. "Can't you just hold it?"

He chuckled. "Rhiannon."

She loved the way he said her name in his low and husky voice. "Oh, all right," she said, sitting up reluctantly. "Any chance you'll let me put you right back?"

She freed his left arm first and he winced as he stretched it out. "No."

"I thought as much." She worked to free the second wrist. "But you seemed to enjoy yourself. I mean, if multiple orgasms are any indication," she added wryly.

The minute he was released, he flipped her over onto her back and pinned her to the bed, stretching her arms up and over her head. "How do you like it?"

"A little rough, as you know," she said silkily, reaching up to lick his throat.

"No," he admitted, then shuddered. "Jeez, woman, you're going to be the death of me."

"Let's hope not," she murmured. She lifted her hips suggestively against him. "That would be a tragedy."

Another gratifying growl vibrated against her lips. "Let's shower," he said. "I want to lather you up and watch the soap bubbles slide over your ass."

"I like the way you think."

He nuzzled her neck, then nosed his way down until he could pull her nipple into his mouth. Wicked sensation whipped through her. "I like the way you taste," he said. "I could easily get addicted. Or become a glutton."

She could, too, Rhiannon thought as her toes

curled into the sheets. And it utterly terrified her. She'd never had any interest in light bondage before, in tying anyone up, and yet she'd wanted control over him, had wanted him to bend to her will and let her have her way with him. There was more going on here than she was willing to admit, most especially to herself. She would acknowledge only that she was seriously besotted with him.

Besotted was a safe word. Anything else…was not.

He tugged her toward the bathroom, adjusted the tap and then followed her in.

Hot water, equally hot man, wonderful naked wet skin…

"Mmm, this is nice," she said as Will filled a washcloth with her soap and rubbed it over her shoulders.

"I love the way this stuff smells," he said. "I'll never look at another orange and not think of you."

She grinned, then turned so that he could wash her chest. "I'll never look at another piece of rope and not think of you."

"You're wicked."

"Yes…but you like it."

"I do." He sighed as though he found the knowledge mystifying.

He turned her around and carefully placed both

of her hands on the shower wall. "I don't have any rope in here, but do you think you could just stand here like this for me? Without moving?"

A breath stuttered out of her lungs. "I'll try."

He ran his hands down her arms, then slowly over her rib cage, casually brushing the sides of her breasts. He continued downward, licking the flute of her spine along the way.

Her legs shook.

He palmed her rump, kissed the twin indentations above her rear, then slowly skimmed her thighs. On the return trek, he pushed his hands around to her front, slipping his fingers over her mound, dipping between her folds, then upward until he held both of her breasts.

Her hands fisted against the shower wall, but she didn't move them. He bent his head and nipped at her neck, the sensitive place where throat met shoulder, and she felt a rush of longing sweep through her. The air was heavy with steam and he was hot and warm at her back and suddenly nothing else mattered. Everything in her world seemed to shift until everything past, present or future was tied to this moment.

He nudged her legs farther apart with his foot, then ducked beneath her arms and kissed his way down her body. He stopped at her sex and though she knew what was coming, she was not prepared for the shock of sensation that burst through her when his fingers parted her curls and his hot tongue laved her clit.

Another tremor made her knees quake and her hands slipped farther down the wall, but didn't leave it.

Then he buried his mouth in her sex, suckling, laving, licking, tormenting her until she was certain she wasn't going to be able to remain on her feet, much less stay anchored to the wall. He slipped a finger deep inside her, hooked it around and massaged a secret spot.

She gasped and locked her knees to keep them in place.

"Will, I can't—"

"Oh, but you will." He chuckled against her. "I did for you. You can for me."

"It's not that I don't want to. I don't know—"

He tented his tongue over her clit and pressed hard, stroking it back and forth, then wrapped an arm around her waist to keep her from falling down. Melting. Disintegrating. Flying apart.

Another skillful sweep of his tongue and a bit of pressure deep inside and she was beating the shower wall with her fist as the orgasm swept her under. She cried out, her voice hoarse and mangled, then literally sagged against him.

Before she could catch her breath, he was suddenly behind her, nudging her folds.

Then he froze and a hot oath fired from between his lips. "I left the condoms in the bedroom."

Oh, hell, no. She needed him inside her. Felt as if she couldn't breathe unless he filled her up again. "I'm clean and on the pill. You?"

"Yes."

"Then what the hell are you waiting for? Get inside me."

The exquisite sensation of him—*just him*—inside of her made unexpected tears prick the backs of her eyes. He felt so good. So perfect. So unbelievably right.

He growled a low purr of masculine satisfaction and his hands bit into her hips. "You are—" He released a shuddered breath as he stilled inside her, seemingly prolonging the moment, observing the event for what it was—flawless. "There aren't words to describe how good you feel to me right now."

He withdrew, then pushed back in.

"I know that f-feeling."

Pushed again, withdrew, a mindless seek and retreat that impossibly made her quicken again. She could feel the tension building in her sex with every skillful stroke of him deep inside her and she lifted her foot and set it on the lip of the tub to give him better access.

He growled and rubbed his hands greedily over her ass, thrust again and again, then carefully pressed his thumb against the rosebud of her bottom.

The sensation was so incredible she heard a loud gasp hiss through the shower and realized it was her own.

"That's…wicked."

"But you like it," he said, tossing the words back at her, and she could hear the self-satisfied smile in his voice.

He pressed harder, upped the tempo and angled deeper. Three crushing plunges later, she shattered. Sound receded, everything went black and white, then suddenly flared into Technicolor focus. She screamed and her nails scraped down the shower wall. A moment later he joined her, his guttural groan alerting her to his impending climax as he pushed in one final time and locked himself in place as though he wanted to permanently cement himself there.

And as the final vestiges of release pulsed through her, she let her hands fall away from the wall…and she let go of that figurative cliff face she'd been clinging to, as well, allowing herself to plummet into that terrifying place she'd never wanted to be.

In love.

Will pressed a kiss to her temple. "Sleep with me," he said.

She did.

13

"YOU'RE THE SECOND PERSON who has come by today and wanted to see those old records," the petite lady told them when Will asked to look at the microfiche. "They're still out," she complained, frowning. "The gentleman—who told me he was a librarian, as well—didn't even bother to put them away. He rushed out of here as if his pants were on fire and hollered an apology."

Will's gaze swung to Rhiannon's and before he could utter a word, she was already firing questions at the woman. "What was he looking at? How long ago did he leave?"

The librarian flinched back at the intensity in Rhiannon's voice and darted a startled look in his direction.

"It's important that we find him," Will said. "He's unwell."

Not exactly a lie. He was diabetic.

She frowned knowingly. "Yes, I could tell that," she told them. "Had to get him a glass of water. The poor man had broken out into a clammy sweat."

The panic in Rhiannon's eyes tore at him.

"Oh, Will," she moaned, her voice cracking. "I knew this. I knew something was wrong. I've had a terrible feeling about it for days now."

"I thought you said you weren't psychic."

"I'm not, but I know when something is wrong," she repeated impatiently. She leaned across the counter to the woman. "How long ago did he leave? This is really important."

The librarian glanced at the clock and fretted as she tried to work it out. "A couple of hours ago," she said. "Maybe longer."

"Can you show me what he was looking at?"

"Right this way," she said. "Follow me."

They were escorted to another dim airless room, where a single book lay on the table. Rhiannon crossed the room quickly and scanned the documents, her gaze darting across the page. It suddenly stopped and she gasped.

"Here it is," she breathed. "Winston Watson. Oh, he was only three," she said, her voice breaking.

"Where was he interred?"

"Creekside Cemetery." She glanced up at the older woman. "Do you know where this is?"

She shook her head. "Your friend asked the same question and I gave him the same answer, honey. I'm sorry."

Will quickly nodded at the woman and propelled Rhiannon toward the exit. "We'll stop and ask until we find it," he told her.

Neither clerk at the first two convenience stores was helpful, but they finally got lucky when they stopped at a local feed and seed store. A couple of old-timers argued over the exact whereabouts long enough to make Rhiannon's face flush with irritation, but finally agreed on the location and passed along the directions.

"How long should it take to get there?" she asked them.

"'Bout fifteen, twenty minutes," one said. "The sign is gone and it's a far piece off the road, so you'll need to keep your eyes open. That's an old one. Not too many people buried there, either."

"I'd like to be buried there," the other one remarked.

"Oh, shut up, Marvin. Charlene's already bought your plot at Morningside."

Marvin frowned. "How do you know that?"

The other man grinned. "Because I sold her the burial insurance."

Marvin harrumphed. "Didn't know she had any."

While they continued to discuss their impending funeral arrangements, Will and Rhiannon hurried back to the Jeep. She tapped her toes impatiently against the floorboard and her mouth was set in a flat, worried line.

"We'll find him."

"Something's wrong," she said. "He would have called me by now."

"He might not have a signal."

She gazed out the window, a line of worry furrowing her brow. "He's had time to get back into town, Will."

He silently agreed, but was playing devil's advocate to try to distract her. "His battery could be dead."

"Stop it," she said. "I know what you're doing. You're worried, too. Don't try to pretend with me, please." She softened her statement with a wan smile.

He reached over and took her hand. "Forgot. Sorry."

And though it seemed bizarre, he *had* forgotten about her talent. Had she picked up on his feelings last night? Will wondered. Had she been able to tell that she'd gone from someone he couldn't resist to someone he suspected he couldn't live without?

A sense of dread settled in his chest as he raced toward what he instinctively knew was the end of this mission. They were going to find Theo today, if not right now, and for the first time Will stopped to consider the impact that was going to have on their present situation.

Mission accomplished. Rhiannon would no doubt insist on driving Theo home, so there would be no point in him hanging around. He would go directly back to Atlanta.

Without her.

To a job that might or might not be his when he told them what had happened.

And he would have to tell them. His conscience wouldn't permit anything less. Regardless of what would happen with her, they still had the right to know that he'd done more than step over the line— he'd ignored it completely.

He peeked at her and wondered what she was thinking. Had her thoughts turned to their inevitable goodbye or was she so preoccupied with finding her mentor that she hadn't even considered what this would mean for them?

For the first time in his life he wished he had some sort of special psychic ability, because he would dearly love to know what was going on in her head. She had to have picked up on how he felt about her—he knew it. She was too perceptive to have missed the change. To have missed his revelation.

But did that affect her? Did she still want something casual? Was she still happy with the status quo? Or like her, had he become her exception?

Tension coiled in his muscles with every rotation of the tires against the pavement, with every mile that put them closer and closer to the end of this journey.

"This is the turnoff," Rhiannon said.

He smoothly wheeled the vehicle onto the small, rutted dirt road. "A mile in, right?"

"Yes." Her tense gaze scanned the road ahead and she nervously wound a lock of hair around her finger.

"He's here," she said. "I can feel him." She closed her eyes and concentrated. Her forehead knotted. "Euphoria and...fear."

Theo must have found the treasure, Will thought. But why was he afraid?

She gasped and leaned forward. "There's his car!"

He'd seen it. The car shot forward as he quickly accelerated down the lane, then jerked to a stop behind Theo's sedan. Rhiannon was out of the car and running toward the graveyard before he could even get the gearshift in Park. He snagged the orange juice he'd been carrying in the cooler from the back, then bolted from the car and ran after Rhiannon.

The cemetery was untended and overgrown with weeds and the weathered headstones—those of them that were still standing—listed sideways as though the effort to remain upright was almost too much to bear.

"Here!" she called, then dropped to her knees, disappearing from sight.

When Will reached her, she'd gathered the old man into her lap and was hugging him tightly. "Theo!" she cried. "Can you hear me? Are you okay?"

A weak smile faltered over his lips. "You know the answer to that, child."

She laughed, but it held a slightly hysterical edge. "Don't toy with me," she said. "Tell me what's wrong!"

"I fainted," he said, his voice low.

Will uncapped the juice and held the bottle up to the older man's mouth. "Drink," he said. "You need the sugar."

Rhiannon's eyes rounded with astonishment, then appreciation. "I wondered why you never drank that," she said absently.

"It wasn't for me." He helped Theo take another drink and was relieved to see a bit of color come into the older man's face. The panic he'd felt when he'd seen Theo unmoving in Rhiannon's arms had been eerily familiar. Terrifyingly so.

"Thank you, young man," Theo rasped. "That's definitely helped. I feel much better." His eager gaze swung to Rhiannon. "But did you see?" he asked her. "Look," he said meaningfully. "It's here, Rhi. *It's here.*"

Her gaze swung to the little headstone that marked Winston Watson's life. Will followed her gaze.

Winston Watson
July 2, 1861
February 19th, 1864
My son, my heart

Ah, Will thought. Theo had been right.

Rhiannon's astonished gaze found his, then Theo's. "Oh, Theo!"

"You've got to dig," he told her. "My tools are right there. I don't have the strength quite yet."

"We've got to get you to a hospital first," she said, her expression clouding. "We'll come back. We'll—"

"Rhiannon," he said. "I've been looking for this for most of my life and have endured years of ridicule over believing in its existence. Do you really think I'm going to leave now without it, when I'm so close? Would you really take this from me?"

"Theo—"

Will picked up the shovel. "Where do I dig?"

Theo's shrewd eyes caught and held his for a minute. He instantly knew what Rhiannon meant about Theo being much better at reading people than she was. He could practically feel the old man excavating his brain. After an interminable moment, Theo smiled up at him. "No time for proper introductions," he said. "We'll do that later." He gestured toward the metal detector. "Hand me that and I'll show you how to work it."

Less than thirty seconds over the grave, the little beeping noise that heralded a find went nuts and Rhiannon marked the ground with the shovel. Will tossed the metal detector aside, snatched the shovel out of her hand and put the blade in the ground. A satisfying thump sounded when the edge of the metal hit something solid.

Theo was able to sit up now. His eyes lit up.

Will quickly removed the earth, then hauled a small metal trunk from the soil. Anticipation chugged through his veins, pushing a smile onto his lips. He walked over and carefully put the box into Theo's withered hands.

The older man slid his fingers lovingly over the box, then withdrew a pocketknife from his khaki pants and used it to pry open the lid. A single torn page lay on top of a blue velvet sack, curiously preserved despite its age.

It was a page from the Bible, the book of Matthew, chapter six.

Theo's hands shook as he carefully handed it over to Rhiannon for her inspection, then he lifted the little pouch from the box.

Diamonds, emeralds, pearls, amethysts, rubies, some in settings, some not, emptied into his open hand and he chortled with glee. "Rhi," he said. "Do you see this?"

Her eyes sparkled with tears and were much prettier than any of the stones in Theo's palm, Will thought.

"I do," she choked out. "You found it." She paused. "And I found you."

"Ah, but I'm no treasure."

"To me you are," she said, wrapping her arm around his shoulders. "Now, let's go."

RHIANNON STEPPED OUT into the hall where Will had patiently waited for hours and an overwhelming sense of loss washed over her before she'd taken the first step in his direction.

It was over.

Though she'd known this moment was going to come and that every step closer to Theo had put her one step closer to their farewell scene, she nevertheless was not prepared for the anguish that felt as if it was shredding her soul.

This was precisely why she hadn't wanted this, Rhiannon thought. Love made you weak. Love made you stupid. And while she knew it was going to hurt now, she was taking a page out of Barney Fife's book and nipping it in the bud.

Time for a clean break.

It would be easier if she knew he wanted it, but…he didn't.

There had been many times in her life when she'd wished she couldn't feel other people's emotions, and last night, when she'd felt Will's attraction and affection shift into something more—something frighteningly significant—she had never been more touched.

Or more miserable.

She could not do this. Didn't want to feel it. She didn't want the roller coaster her parents had. Didn't want the misery that went along with the joy.

Her hands shook as she started toward him and she made herself smile.

Will pushed away from the wall as she approached. She could feel the wariness hovering around him. He knew what was coming. She probed his emotions and mentally gave a sigh of relief when she felt his resignation.

He would not fight.

Because, ultimately, he was a gentleman.

"You didn't have to wait," she said, spying her suitcase at his feet. "We've been back there for hours."

"I wanted to wait," he said. "Wanted to make sure he was going to be okay."

"He's almost fully recovered," she said. "He's been properly frightened, so I think he'll take better care of himself in the future." She smiled at him. "You were great back there. Without the orange juice and hard candy, he might not have been so lucky."

"But he's going to be fine?"

"Yes," she said. "Insulin dependent, much to his horror, but fine."

He released a pent-up breath. "That's a relief.

"You know I'll have to give Tad an update," he added, darting her an uncertain look. "Does Theo want him to know about the jewels?"

"Oh, yes." Rhiannon felt her smile widen. "Since he never believed they existed, Theo is making sure he doesn't get them."

Will chuckled. "Can't say that I blame him."

"Tad's in for another surprise, too," she said, chuckling. "Theo's made a few changes in his will that are certain to enrage his son. But the city council will be *very* happy."

"Serves him right," Will said with a grimace. "Greed makes people mean and stupid."

Rhiannon couldn't agree more. She crossed her arms over her chest, trying to hold it together. "So...you'll be heading back to Atlanta, right?"

His guarded gaze tangled with hers. "That's the plan. I'm assuming you'll be driving Theo back to Begonia?"

She nodded. "I will. We should be able to leave in the morning."

"Good."

The silence lengthened between them and she swallowed, preparing her heart for the break. "Thank you so much," she said shakily. "Particularly for letting me come along with you."

He merely shrugged and that smile she'd come to love tugged at the corner of his mouth. "It's a good thing you did. I couldn't have found him without you."

She nodded primly. "I told you I would be helpful."

"A helpful distraction," he corrected, and it seemed like a lifetime ago that they'd had this argument. "But a—" his gaze drifted over her mouth "—very welcome one," he finished, his voice curiously rusty.

And it cleaved her heart in two. Rhiannon actually thought she felt it break.

She grabbed her bag. "I'm actually going to go try and clean up a bit," she told him, gesturing toward the restroom. She leaned forward on her tippy toes and gave him an awkward, one-armed hug. His own familiar arms twined around her waist and squeezed.

"I'm going to duck in and tell Theo goodbye, if that's all right."

She nodded, swallowing thickly. "I'm sure he'd like that."

He hesitated. "Rhiannon—"

"It's okay," she said before he could finish. "The status quo, remember?"

His face was grim, but he nodded all the same. He walked around her, thankfully without saying goodbye—unbearable—and soon disappeared into Theo's room.

Rhiannon looked heavenward, hoping to stem the tears that suddenly stung the backs of her eyes.

"This is for the best," she muttered quietly. "Really."

Too bad she wasn't convinced.

14

"AH, MR. FORRESTER," Theo enthused as Will walked into his hospital room. "Rhiannon tells me you're the security expert my son hired to find me."

Will nodded, still trying to process what had just happened out in the hall. He'd known it was coming, of course. But knowing it and being prepared to accept it were two entirely different things.

But he didn't have a choice.

She didn't want him.

He'd known that going in and had been fine with it until his feelings had changed.

He nodded at the older gentleman, a sense of pride swelling in his chest that he'd actually helped him, that he hadn't been too late. A curious sense of redemption lightened his heart, making his shoulders feel a little less heavy. "I am, sir. But

I couldn't have found you without Rhiannon," he told him. "You really gave her quite a scare."

"I know and I truly regret that. I'd meant to call her later and let her know what I'd found, but I forgot to pack the charger on my cell phone and didn't want to call collect. That would have been rude."

Will started to point out that she would have been much happier with a collect phone call than being left in the dark, but didn't. What was the point? A thought pricked.

"What exactly was it that you did find?" he asked. "Rhiannon didn't think you knew about Mortimer's first family."

His faded eyes lit up. "A photograph of the three of them," Theo told him. "Tucked in one of Mortimer's old Bibles. It was probably the only one that Sophia never destroyed. On the back was the inscription 'My love and my heart.'"

Will inclined his head. "Very clever."

"It was worth it," Theo said, nodding. "Not because of the jewels, you understand, but because of the mystery and the history behind them."

"They're probably worth a fortune."

His eyes sparkled with mischief. "My son will salivate."

Theo pulled the little bag from beneath his hip

and emptied it onto the tray table, and Will was struck again by how lovely the jewels were.

The older man plucked a single diamond solitaire from the pile and held it up for Will's inspection. "Rhiannon will like this one."

He wouldn't know, Will thought, swallowing.

"When were you planning on telling her you're in love with her?"

Will blinked and his startled gaze found Theo's. He laughed uncomfortably. "I'm sorry?"

Theo's brows formed a bushy line. "Don't play coy. You're talking to a master. I'm sure you know that."

He did. "Does she know?"

"Probably."

Damn.

"Has she given you that rubbish about being content in her own company and how love makes people stupid and how she doesn't want any part of it?"

Will laughed at the distaste in Theo's voice. "In a manner of speaking, yes."

Theo frowned. "Hogwash," he retorted. "Rhi's so used to feeling the bad things that come along with love that she's afraid of it. She focuses so much on how the emotion tears one down that she's ignored how it can build you up." Theo's gaze burned with intensity. "It's the most powerful, humbling emotion of them all. She calls it the Boss."

She would, Will thought with another weak chuckle. He rubbed the back of his neck. "She knows where I am if she wants to find me," he said. "I'm not going to force her."

Theo grew thoughtful. "No, she'll have to come around on her own. But she will. She loves you, too, you know."

Hope flared pathetically. "She does?"

"Yes, she just hasn't fully admitted it herself yet. But when she does—" he pressed the solitaire into Will's hand "—you're going to need this."

Will's mouth opened, but he couldn't get any words to come out. He cleared his throat. "Sir, I can't accept this. It's—"

"It's yours. For *your* treasure."

Will shook his head and silently pocketed the stone. "I'll return it if you're wrong."

Theo merely smiled. "I'm never wrong."

He certainly hoped so, Will thought. He had a lot riding on the outcome.

"THIS IS RIDICULOUS," Elizabeth said two weeks later as Rhiannon continued to mope around her house. "You can't keep on like this. It isn't healthy."

"I know," she said glumly. "Love sucks. This is why I didn't want it."

"Whether you wanted it or not, Rhi, you've got it." She scratched Keno behind the ears. "I wish I could understand why you don't simply call him."

"Because that would change the status quo, the one I told him I wanted."

"But isn't he in love with you, too?" Elizabeth asked, seemingly confused.

Rhiannon flinched at the word. "I think so. Theo says definitely and has been lecturing me about how fabulous love can be and how I've just got a terrible attitude." She grimaced. "Can you believe he actually told me he was disappointed in me?"

Liz snorted. "Yes, I can. He's an opinionated old fart."

"He is not," Rhiannon admonished, even though her friend was only kidding. "He's just looking at everything through Sarah-colored glasses. He had a wonderful, healthy relationship with her and doesn't understand why I'm reluctant to hand my happiness over to another person."

"Your parents were pretty screwed up," Elizabeth conceded. "But that doesn't mean you and Will would be. History isn't doomed to repeat itself. Just look at how different Theo and Tad are."

Tad, Rhiannon thought sourly. She absolutely couldn't believe him. Now that his father had found the Watson treasure, he was determined to get back into her good graces in order to get her to convince Theo to leave the jewels to him.

Er...no. When hell freezes over. Idiot.

But it was an interesting turn of events, one she had to admit she was enjoying.

And to a degree, logically, Rhiannon knew Liz was right. But she was still terrified of falling in love only to fall on her face. To have it backfire. She didn't want to be one of those bitter old people she saw consumed with the one who had gotten away, or the one who had broken their heart, or the one who had died.

It inevitably ended in disaster, even in Theo's case, which she had, in a fit of irritation, pointed out. Her old friend's eyes had softened and he'd taken her hand. "Rhi, there isn't a day that goes by that I don't miss my Sarah. But even knowing what I feel now, I would walk through hell for the simple pleasure of getting to hold her hand again. You don't know what you're missing, and it pains me that you're too afraid to try."

Was he right? Rhiannon wondered. Was she being a coward? Was fear what was holding her back?

All she knew was that it felt as if a huge part of

her chest was missing and it was all she could do to put one unhappy foot in front of the other every day.

Initially she'd told herself it would get better. That time was the ultimate remedy. That she would be fine. But she was increasingly afraid that this hole in her middle was getting bigger, the edges becoming more raw. She'd looked at her toothpaste yesterday, thought of him and stood in her bathroom and squalled.

She was falling apart.

Will, undoubtedly, could put her back together. But would he keep her that way? Or would he break her heart? That was what terrified her. That was what held her back.

"Go to him," Elizabeth said. "Tell him you want to change the status quo." Her eyes twinkled. "Then tie him to the bed again."

Rhiannon blushed and rolled her eyes. "Why in the hell did I tell you that?"

"Because we don't have any secrets," her friend said. "Trust me, Rhi. This is right. Don't waste it."

"But what if it ends badly?"

"But what if it doesn't end at all?"

An image of Will, shorn hair, pale gray eyes and that endearing smile, rose in her mind's eye, tormenting her with its perfection. She ached for him. Still burned for him. Dreamed of him every night.

Rhiannon released a pent-up breath and stood. "Okay," she said. "Time to change the status quo."

And she was going to need to stop by the hardware store on her way out of town.

"RHIANNON PALMER just came into the office, asking about Will," McCann informed Payne and Flanagan with a huge smile on his face.

"What did you tell her?" Payne asked, his antennae twitching. Will had been a dozen kinds of miserable since his return and had owned up to the relationship with Rhiannon. That took courage, character and a sense of right and wrong that wasn't always a part of every man's makeup. And Payne could hardly criticize Will for it when each and every one of them was guilty of the exact same offense.

"I pointed her in the direction of his apartment, of course," McCann said. "She lives close enough that he can commute. If she'd been any farther out of Atlanta, though, I might not have been so helpful. We can't keep losing our help."

Jamie laughed. "What's she look like?"

"Not half as beautiful as my wife," McCann said

dutifully. "But she's gorgeous. Pretty eyes. Violet-blue."

"You going to write a poem about her?" Jamie teased.

"Go to hell," McCann said, chuckling.

"I hope this ends well," Payne said.

"She's here, isn't she?" Jamie pointed out.

"She is," McCann said. He frowned. "And she had a length of rope sticking out of her purse."

MAYBE HE'D GET A DOG, Will thought as he sat in his silent apartment. The television was on, tuned to a baseball game, but he hadn't so much as looked at the score. He needed a companion of some sort. Granted, the Triumvirate had realized he'd sunk into a terrible funk and had been trying to jar him out of it—and he genuinely appreciated it—but at the end of the day, both McCann and Payne went home to their wives, and Jamie went to his apartment to talk on the phone half the night with his.

Though Will had had work over the past couple of weeks, it had been nothing that had taken him out of Atlanta and nothing that had required he use more than half his brain.

Which was good, because the other half was always consumed with Rhiannon.

Even thinking her name made an ache build up his chest. Maybe she had it right about the Boss, he thought, chuckling at her nickname for love. Maybe love did make people stupid and reckless and weak. Maybe she'd been onto something with her status quo.

And maybe this was all bullshit and he was just miserable, Will thought, rubbing the bridge of his nose.

But it had to get better. He couldn't possibly feel like this forever. As if he'd left a part of himself in Virginia and it had migrated south to Begonia, Georgia.

A brisk knock sounded at his door, which was odd because McCann and Flanagan typically just walked in. Must be Payne, Will thought, pushing up from his recliner and making his way to the door. He pulled it open and drew up short.

Rhiannon.

He blinked, wondering if his pathetic imagination was playing tricks on him.

"Hi, Will," she said, smiling tentatively. "Are you busy?"

He cleared his throat and marveled at the joy just looking at her made him feel. He felt a smile drift over his lips and hoped he didn't look like a fool.

But he was her fool.

"No," he said, opening the door wider. "Come in."

She walked by him, bringing the scent of

oranges with her, and his mouth instantly watered. She wore a red sleeveless top and another one of those little flippy skirts that had made it so easy to take her wherever he'd wanted. If she didn't have on any panties, he was going to have a stroke.

She settled on the side of his couch and waited for him to resume his spot in his recliner before she finally spoke.

"How have you been?"

"You read me the minute I opened the door," he said. "I'm sure you know."

"Depressed, lonely, miserable?" she asked, wincing.

He chuckled darkly. "That about sums it up."

"I can help you with that," she said, and there was a hint of uncertainty behind the bravado, which alerted him to how much this was costing her.

But it had to be her move. And he'd be a liar if he said he wasn't enjoying watching her make it.

He quirked a brow. "You can?"

She lifted her chin. "Definitely. And I would be more than willing to distract you, as well. It's just part of the services I offer."

His lips twitched. "What about the status quo?" he asked, letting her know that this wasn't going to be on some trial basis. She had to give him all or nothing. Anything less would result in him being in a padded room devoid of sharp objects.

She shrugged as though it didn't matter. "Time to change it, don't you think?"

"I was ready to change it before we left Virginia."

She smiled sadly. "I was afraid, Will. But I'm trying to be brave now. Is that going to count for anything?"

"You off your game?" he asked. "Surely you know the answer to that already."

She smiled and ducked her head. "I have an idea."

"Then why are you still sitting over there?"

She launched herself at him. The breath whooshed out of his lungs and into her mouth and her fingers were suddenly in his hair, kneading his scalp, then lovingly—reverently—tracing the lines of his face.

"I've missed you so much," she said, straddling him.

Will slid his palms over her bare ass and smiled against her lips. "No panties."

"No point in wearing them around you." She kissed him again, pressing her sweet breasts against his chest, and it took all the strength he possessed to push her back. He had to do something first.

"I've got something for you," he said, reaching into his pocket. He withdrew the ring and held it up for her inspection.

Her eyes rounded and she gasped. "Will." She looked closer. "That looks awfully familiar. Where have I—" Another sharp inhalation. "The Watson treasure? But how did you— Theo," she said meaningfully.

"He gave it to me for you," he said. "Because he wasn't the only person who found his treasure on that trip. I did, too. I'm in love with you, Rhiannon. And I don't care if it scares the hell out of you." He chuckled softly. "Welcome to my world."

"Are you going to put it on my hand?" she asked.

His chest felt as if it would explode with pride. "Happily."

She admired the stone on her finger. "I've got something for your hand, too," she said, and there was a hint of something wicked in her smile. She reached into her purse and pulled out a length of rope, then wagged it at him significantly.

He laughed, astonished, and offered his wrist. "Bind me," he said. Because he was always going to be her love slave.

She wrapped the rope around his wrist, then around her own and held it up meaningfully. "We're bound."

"Ah." Will sighed as he freed himself from his jeans and pushed into her. *Home,* he thought. "I like this better." He nuzzled her neck. "It's got endless possibilities."

She laughed. "I didn't know you were psychic."

"I knew you'd be back, didn't I?"

"That confident, were you?"

"No," he corrected. "Just hopeful…."

* * * * *

HARLEQUIN® *Blaze*™

COMING NEXT MONTH

Available June 29, 2010

#549 BORN ON THE 4TH OF JULY
Jill Shalvis, Rhonda Nelson, Karen Foley

#550 AMBUSHED!
Vicki Lewis Thompson
Sons of Chance

#551 THE BRADDOCK BOYS: BRENT
Kimberly Raye
Love at First Bite

#552 THE TUTOR
Hope Tarr
Blaze Historicals

#553 MY FAKE FIANCÉE
Nancy Warren
Forbidden Fantasies

#554 SIMON SAYS...
Donna Kauffman
The Wrong Bed

REQUEST YOUR FREE BOOKS!

2 FREE NOVELS
PLUS 2
FREE GIFTS!

HARLEQUIN®

Blaze™

Red-hot reads!

HB10R

HARLEQUIN®

A *Romance*

FOR EVERY MOOD™

Spotlight on
Heart & Home

Heartwarming romances
where love can happen
right when you least expect it.

See the next page to enjoy a sneak peek
from Silhouette Special Edition®,
a Heart and Home series.

CATHHSSE10

Introducing McFARLANE'S PERFECT BRIDE
by USA TODAY bestselling author Christine Rimmer,
from Silhouette Special Edition®.

Entranced. Captivated. Enchanted.

Connor sat across the table from Tori Jones and couldn't help thinking that those words exactly described what effect the small-town schoolteacher had on him. He might as well stop trying to tell himself he wasn't interested. He was powerfully drawn to her.

Clearly, he should have dated more when he was younger.

There had been a couple of other women since Jennifer had walked out on him. But he had never been entranced. Or captivated. Or enchanted.

Until now.

He wanted her—*her,* Tori Jones, in particular. Not just someone suitably attractive and well-bred, as Jennifer had been. Not just someone sophisticated, sexually exciting and discreet, which pretty much described the two women he'd dated after his marriage crashed and burned.

It came to him that he...he *liked* this woman. And that was new to him. He liked her quick wit, her wisdom and her big heart. He liked the passion in her voice when she talked about things she believed in.

He liked *her.* And suddenly it mattered all out of proportion that she might like him, too.

Was he losing it? He couldn't help but wonder. Was he cracking under the strain—of the soured economy, the McFarlane House setbacks, his divorce, the scary changes in his son? Of the changes he'd decided he needed to make in his life and himself?

Strangely, right then, on his first date with Tori Jones, he didn't care if he just might be going over the edge. He was having a great time—having *fun*, of all things—and he didn't want it to end.

Is Connor finally able to admit his feelings to Tori, and are they reciprocated?
Find out in McFARLANE'S PERFECT BRIDE
by USA TODAY *bestselling author Christine Rimmer.*
Available July 2010,
only from Silhouette Special Edition®.

HARLEQUIN *Presents*

Bestselling Harlequin Presents® author

Penny Jordan

brings you an exciting new trilogy...

Needed:
THE WORLD'S MOST
ELIGIBLE
BILLIONAIRES

Three penniless sisters:
how far will they go to save the ones they love?

Lizzie, Charley and Ruby refuse to drown in their debts.
And three of the richest, most ruthless men in the world
are about to enter their lives. Pure, proud but penniless,
how far will these sisters go to save the ones they love?

Look out for

Lizzie's story—THE WEALTHY GREEK'S
CONTRACT WIFE, July

Charley's story—THE ITALIAN DUKE'S
VIRGIN MISTRESS, August

Ruby's story—MARRIAGE: TO CLAIM HIS TWINS,
September

www.eHarlequin.com

HP12927